# Dear Parents:

Congratulations! Your child is taking the first steps on an exciting journey. The destination? Independent reading!

**STEP INTO READING**® will help your child get there. The program offers five steps to reading success. Each step includes fun stories and colorful art or photographs. In addition to original fiction and books with favorite characters, there are Step into Reading Non-Fiction Readers, Phonics Readers and Boxed Sets, Sticker Readers, and Comic Readers—a complete literacy program with something to interest every child.

## Learning to Read, Step by Step!

**Ready to Read**  **Preschool–Kindergarten**
• big type and easy words • rhyme and rhythm • picture clues
For children who know the alphabet and are eager to begin reading.

**Reading with Help**  **Preschool–Grade 1**
• basic vocabulary • short sentences • simple stories
For children who recognize familiar words and sound out new words with help.

**Reading on Your Own**  **Grades 1–3**
• engaging characters • easy-to-follow plots • popular topics
For children who are ready to read on their own.

**Reading Paragraphs**  **Grades 2–3**
• challenging vocabulary • short paragraphs • exciting stories
For newly independent readers who read simple sentences with confidence.

**Ready for Chapters**  **Grades 2–4**
• chapters • longer paragraphs • full-color art
For children who want to take the plunge into chapter books but still like colorful pictures.

**STEP INTO READING**® is designed to give every child a successful reading experience. The grade levels are only guides; children will progress through the steps at their own speed, developing confidence in their reading.

Remember, a lifetime love of reading starts with a single step!

Published in the United States by Random House Children's Books, a division of Penguin Random House LLC, 1745 Broadway, New York, NY 10019, and in Canada by Penguin Random House Canada Limited, Toronto.

Step into Reading, Random House, and the Random House colophon are registered trademarks of Penguin Random House LLC.

Visit us on the Web!
StepIntoReading.com
rhcbooks.com

Educators and librarians, for a variety of teaching tools, visit us at RHTeachersLibrarians.com

ISBN 978-1-5247-7238-3 (trade) — ISBN 978-1-5247-7239-0 (lib. bdg.)

Printed in the United States of America
10 9 8 7 6 5 4 3 2 1

# Sisters Save the Day!

adapted by Kristen L. Depken
based on the original screenplay
by Grant Moran

Random House New York

One day,

Barbie's dad has an idea.

Family time travel!

They will pretend to go back in time.
They will pretend to be pioneers!

That means no cars,
phones,
or electronics.

Skipper does *not*
like that.

Everyone else
is excited.
They try to change
Skipper's mind.
Skipper says yes.

Barbie and her family
set up a campsite
in the backyard.

They have tents
for sleeping.
They have a fire pit
for cooking.

Ken comes
to take pictures.
He brings a phone
for emergencies.

The girls turn
off their phones.
"Nooo!"
cries Skipper.

The family gets used
to pioneer life.
Barbie and Skipper
wash dishes by hand.

Chelsea and Stacie

play a clapping game.

At night, 🎵

the girls get bored.

Barbie teaches
them a song.
They have fun!

Oh no!
It starts
to rain.

The girls go
inside their tent.
The tent is leaking!
They are not happy.

The next morning,
Barbie and Skipper
walk to a farm
to get milk.
The milk is heavy.

The girls ride home
on the farm horse,
Misty.

They are very tired
when they get back!

Stacie and Chelsea
are tired, too.

Just then,
Barbie's mom gets
an emergency call.

Her work needs

a special project ⭐

right away.

There is too much traffic

to get it to the office

in time.

Barbie has an idea.
She and Skipper
will ride Misty
to their mom's work.

Pioneers did not
have traffic.
They will not
have traffic either!

The girls take
the project and ride
to the office.
They ride
up the escalator.

They ride
in the elevator.

They get the project
to the boss in time!

"Thank you!"
says their mom
when they get home.

Barbie, Skipper,
and Misty
saved the day!

# Pioneer life is not so bad after all!

# Apple-Berry Tapioca Pudding

*A lovely, light way to end a meal. This pudding is just as good warm as chilled,
so you can make and enjoy it on short notice.*

1¼ cups unsweetened apple juice

1 cup pureed raspberries, strained, or strawberries

¼ cup quick-cooking tapioca

1–2 tablespoons honey (optional)

IN A SAUCEPAN, combine the juice, raspberries or strawberries, tapioca, and honey if using. Let stand for 5 to 10 minutes. Bring to a boil over medium heat, stirring often. When mixture reaches a full boil, remove from heat, and allow to cool for about 20 minutes.

Stir well, and serve warm or chilled.

*Makes 4 or 5 servings*

## Variation

*Apple Tapioca Pudding:* Omit the berries and use 2¼ cups apple juice and, if desired, 2 tablespoons apple juice concentrate.

# Pineapple Pudding

*A delicious pudding made without sugar or milk.*

16 ounces firm tofu

½ cup thawed pineapple juice concentrate

3 tablespoons light agave nectar or honey

2 tablespoons walnut oil

1 can (20 ounces) crushed pineapple

¼ cup chopped walnuts (optional)

DRAIN THE TOFU for 20 to 30 minutes, pressing it between cotton towels to extract as much moisture as possible. Crumble with a fork.

Place the juice concentrate in a blender. Add the tofu, ⅓ at a time, and process until smooth after each addition, stopping to scrape the container as necessary. With the blender running, slowly add the honey and oil. Blend well and pour into a bowl.

Drain the pineapple and reserve the juice for another use. Stir into the tofu mixture. Chill for at least 1 hour. Spoon into individual serving dishes. Top each serving with chopped walnuts if using.

*Makes 6 servings*

---

### COOK'S TIP

∗ Boil the pineapple juice concentrate for 2 minutes to destroy the enzymes that may cause a burning sensation in your mouth.

---

# Vanilla Rice Pudding

*This is a great old-fashioned dessert—and so nourishing
we sometimes have it for breakfast!*

¾ **cup short-grain rice**

1½ **cups water**

½ **teaspoon salt**

2 **cups nut or soy milk**

⅓ **cup light agave nectar or honey**

2 **tablespoons tapioca starch or
arrowroot**

1½ **teaspoons vanilla extract**

IN A 2-QUART SAUCEPAN, combine the
rice, water, and salt. Cover and cook for 40
minutes, or until the rice is very tender and
water is mostly absorbed.

Add 1½ cups of the milk and the agave
nectar or honey, and cook, stirring, over
medium heat. Dissolve the tapioca or arrowroot in the remaining ½ cup of milk.

Bring the rice mixture to a boil and stir
in the tapioca-milk mixture. Cook, stirring,
over medium heat for 3 minutes, or until
the mixture thickens. Boil for 1 to 2 minutes more. Remove from the heat and let
cool for 20 to 30 minutes. Stir in the vanilla.

Serve warm or chilled. Cover and refrigerate for up to 5 days.

*Makes 8 servings*

---
COOK'S TIPS
---

✳ If you like, you can also use rice or goat's milk.

✳ Another sweetener that's very tasty here is maple
  syrup.

# Fancy Parfaits

*Here's a simple way to dress up a humble pudding.*

**Apple-Berry Tapioca Pudding (page
333) or Pineapple Pudding (page 333)**

2 **cups Whipped Tofu Topping
(page 346) or Nutty Crème Topping
(page 345)**

1 **cup chopped toasted almonds
(optional)**

ALTERNATE LAYERS of pudding and topping in chilled parfait glasses, ending with
the topping. Sprinkle with the nuts if using.

*Makes 8 servings*

---
COOK'S TIP
---

✳ May serve immediately or chill for up to 8 hours.

# Lime Bavarian

*This grand and elegant dessert is wonderfully easy. It's light and airy, yet free of eggs and cream. Best made in season with fresh, ripe honeydew.*

½ cup cashews
¾ cup boiling water
1 small honeydew, cut into chunks
2 tablespoons unflavored gelatin
¼ cup honey
⅓ cup lime juice

OIL A 1-QUART MOLD.

Place the cashews in a blender and process until finely ground. Add the water, and process at high speed for 2 minutes, or until smooth. Pour into a stainless steel bowl, and place in freezer to chill.

Place the melon, a few chunks at a time, in the blender and process until smooth to make 3 cups of puree. Pour ½ cup into a small saucepan. Sprinkle with the gelatin and allow to soften for 5 minutes. Heat briefly to dissolve gelatin. Stir in the honey. Cool to room temperature.

Add the lime juice to the puree remaining in the blender. With the blender running, pour in the cashew mixture. Pour in the gelatin mixture. Process for 30 seconds more.

Pour into the prepared mold. Chill for 8 hours or overnight. Unmold to serve.

***Makes about 6 servings***

# Quick and Easy Banana Dessert

2 large, ripe bananas
¼ cup chopped pecans
2–3 tablespoons maple syrup

CUT THE BANANAS in half lengthwise. Cut each piece in half crosswise.

Mist a nonstick skillet with cooking spray and add the bananas and nuts. Cook, without turning, over medium heat for 5 minutes, or until the bananas are lightly browned on bottom and heated through. Drizzle with the maple syrup and heat for 1 minute more. Serve warm.

***Makes 2 servings***

# Poached Pear Melba

*This is fancier than plain fresh fruit yet takes only minutes to prepare.*

4 large pears, halved, cored, and peeled

1½ cups unsweetened pineapple juice

1 cup raspberries

1–2 tablespoons honey

Pinch of unbuffered vitamin C crystals (optional)

PLACE THE PEARS and juice in a 3-quart saucepan, and cook for 12 to 15 minutes, or just until tender. Using a slotted spoon, remove the pears to a bowl. Cover and keep warm. Reserve the juice for another use.

Place the raspberries in a blender, and process until pureed. Strain through a sieve, pressing to extract all the juice. Stir in the honey to taste. Add the vitamin C to taste (for tang).

To serve, place 2 pear halves on a dessert plate. Top with raspberry sauce. Serve warm or cold.

***Makes 4 servings***

## Variation

*Poached Pears with Pineapple Sauce:* Omit the raspberries. After removing the pears from the poaching liquid, reduce the liquid to about 1 cup. Stir in the honey, omitting the vitamin C. Dissolve 1 tablespoon arrowroot in 2 tablespoons cool juice or water, and stir into the sauce. Cook, stirring constantly, for 1 to 2 minutes, or until thick and clear. Serve warm.

---
### COOK'S TIP
---

✻ To double the recipe, poach the pears in batches.

# Fancy Berries and Nuts

*Patterned after that international favorite, strawberries Romanoff,*
*this dessert uses less allergenic berries and dispenses with the traditional cream.*
*Though simple, this makes an elegant dessert.*

1½ cups blueberries

1½ cups raspberries

2–4 tablespoons light agave nectar

  Nutty Crème Topping, chilled
  (page 345)

¼ cup chopped walnuts (optional)

DIVIDE THE BLUEBERRIES and raspberries among chilled serving bowls. Drizzle each with 1 tablespoon agave nectar. Top with Nutty Crème Topping and some nuts if using.

*Makes about 4 servings*

### Variation

*Fancy Fruit and Nuts:* Replace the berries with sliced peaches, plums, nectarines, apricots, or bananas.

---

### COOK'S TIPS

* To limit this dessert to two food families (Plum and Cactus) use peaches, nectarines, or apricots as the fruit, almonds for the nuts, and light agave nectar for the sweetener in the topping.

* If you want, use other favorite nuts in this recipe.

# English Trifle

*Trifle is traditionally made with ladyfingers soaked in rum, egg custard, fruit, jelly, and*
*whipped cream. This wonderful facsimile uses no wheat, cream, or eggs but is just as delightful.*

12 thin Grain-Free Pancakes (page 89)

 1 cup Apricot Topping (page 346)

4–8 teaspoons thawed apple or white
  grape juice concentrate

 ¼ cup chopped toasted almonds

 ¾ cup Almond Dessert Sauce, chilled
  (page 347) (optional)

AT LEAST 6 HOURS AHEAD of serving time, arrange 4 pancakes next to each other on a large serving platter (or individually on 4 dessert dishes). Spread each with about ¼" of apricot topping. Add a second pancake, and spread with more topping. Top with a third pancake. Drizzle 1 to 2 teaspoons of the juice concentrate over each stack. Cover with plastic wrap, waxed paper, or cellophane, and chill for at least 6 hours.

At serving time, use any remaining apricot topping to top each stack. Sprinkle with the almonds. Surround each stack of pancakes with the almond dessert sauce if using.

*Makes 4 servings*

# Molded Grape Gel

*Dress this up or down for a light buffet dessert.*

3 tablespoons unflavored gelatin

1 cup cool water

½ cup raw cashews

⅓ cup boiling water

1 can (12 ounces) purple grape juice concentrate

1½ cups water

1 tablespoon lemon juice or ¼ teaspoon unbuffered vitamin C crystals (optional)

OIL A 5-CUP MOLD.

In a small saucepan, sprinkle the gelatin over the cool water, and allow to soften for a few minutes. Heat briefly to dissolve the gelatin, and let cool to lukewarm.

Place the cashews in a blender and process until ground to a fine powder. Add the boiling water, and process for 1 minute. Add the juice concentrate, and process on high speed for 2 minutes. Add the 1½ cups water, and process briefly on low speed to mix.

With the blender on low, add the gelatin mixture. Add the lemon juice or vitamin C if using to taste (for tang).

Pour into the prepared mold. Chill until firm. Unmold before serving.

***Makes 5 cups***

---

COOK'S TIP

* If you want, you can use individual glasses or dishes instead of the 5-cup mold.

## Variations

*Molded Pineapple Gel:* Replace the grape juice concentrate with pineapple juice concentrate. Boil for 3 minutes, and let cool before proceeding with recipe.

*Grape Salad Squares:* Chill the gelatin mixture just until it begins to thicken. Fold in diced fruit. Pour into an oiled 13" × 9" baking dish. Chill until firm.

# Peach-Almond Ice Cream

*A nondairy ice cream that's also free of soy, and only involves two food families.*

½ cup ground almonds

1 cup boiling water

½ cup light agave nectar or honey

2 tablespoons almond oil

1 teaspoon vanilla extract (optional)

¼–½ teaspoon almond extract

4 peaches, sliced

CHILL 6 DISHES.

In a blender, combine the almonds and water. Process for 1 minute. With the blender running, add the agave nectar or honey, oil, vanilla if using, and almond extract. Transfer to a small stainless steel bowl, and place in the freezer to chill.

Place the peaches in the blender, and process until pureed. Add the cooled almond mixture and process until smooth.

Pour into an 8" × 8" or 9" × 9" baking dish. Freeze until solid. Cut into 1" cubes, and place, half at a time, in the blender. Process until pureed to the consistency of soft ice cream.

Serve immediately in the prepared dishes.

*Makes 6 servings*

# Banana-Fudge Sundaes

*This is a great stand-in for ice cream at birthday parties.*
*Yet it's easy enough to make regularly for the family.*

1 **frozen banana, thinly sliced**
¼ **cup Fudge Fondue for Fruit, chilled (page 349)**

DIVIDE THE BANANA between 2 dessert dishes. Top each portion with 2 tablespoons of Fudge Fondue for Fruit. Serve at once.

*Makes 2 servings*

# Banana Sherbet

*Very easy, very simple, and very good.*

3 **tablespoons frozen white grape or apple juice concentrate, or water**
1 **tablespoon lemon juice or ¼ teaspoon unbuffered vitamin C crystals**
2 **large frozen bananas, sliced ¾" thick**

CHILL 2 DISHES.

In a blender, combine the juice concentrate or water, lemon juice or vitamin C, and a few of the banana slices. Process until pureed. Add the remaining banana, a few slices at a time, and process for 7 to 8 minutes, or until the mixture is the consistency of soft-serve ice cream, stopping to scrape the sides of the container as necessary.

Serve immediately in the prepared dishes.

*Makes 2 servings*

# Soft Sherbet

*A refreshing, sugar-free sherbet.*

1 can (8 ounces) crushed unsweetened pineapple, packed in juice

1½ cups frozen strawberries or bananas cut into 1" chunks

1–2 tablespoons light agave nectar or maple syrup

CHILL 4 DISHES.

Place the pineapple with juice in a stainless steel bowl. Place in the freezer for 1 hour, until chilled but not yet frozen. Pour into a blender and process for 30 seconds.

With the blender running, add the berries or bananas, 2 or 3 at a time, and process until pureed, stopping to scrape the sides of the container as necessary. Add the agave nectar or maple syrup to taste and process until blended.

Serve immediately in the prepared dishes.

***Makes 4 servings***

---

### COOK'S TIP

✳ To double the recipe, make the sherbet in 2 separate batches. Place the first batch in a bowl in the freezer while you make the second, but do not allow it to freeze solid.

# All-Fruit Sorbet

*The consistency of this cool, refreshing dessert is that of soft-serve ice cream that will barely hold a curl on top. I make this after we've eaten, right before we're ready to enjoy it, but if you like your sorbet a little firmer, whip it up 30 to 60 minutes before you're ready to serve it.*

1–2 tablespoons apple or white grape juice or juice concentrate

1 tablespoon canola oil

1½ cups frozen fruit chunks: peaches, nectarines, plums

IN A BLENDER, combine the juice or juice concentrate, oil, and frozen fruit, 2 or 3 chunks at a time, and process on high until smooth.

***Makes 2 servings***

---

### COOK'S TIPS

✳ Feel free to use other juices or juice concentrates.

✳ Don't double this recipe; make separate batches instead. Keep the prepared sorbet in the freezer while making more.

✳ Other excellent candidates for this sorbet include berries, pitted fruits such as apricots and cherries, seedless grapes, drained canned pineapple chunks, and bananas. Use singularly or in combination.

# Simple-Simon Pineapple Sorbet

*This refreshing dessert is incredibly quick and easy to make.*

1 can (20 ounces) crushed pineapple, frozen

1–2 tablespoons frozen pineapple juice concentrate

CHILL 4 DISHES.

Remove the top and bottom from the can of pineapple. Push out the fruit. On a cutting board and using a chef's knife, cut into 4 circles. Cut each circle into quarters.

In a blender, combine the juice concentrate and pineapple, 4 pieces at a time, and process at medium-to-high speed for 6 to 8 minutes, stopping occasionally to scrape down the sides of the container.

Serve immediately in chilled dishes.

***Makes 4 servings***

# Carob Frosting

*This delicious frosting looks too sinfully rich to be good for you.*
*But it's all "good stuff" and the perfect icing for a birthday cake.*

8 ounces firm tofu, drained and cut into 1" cubes

2–3 tablespoons light agave nectar or honey

2–3 tablespoons carob powder

1½ tablespoons walnut or sunflower oil

2 tablespoons smooth almond or cashew butter

1 teaspoon vanilla extract

¼ teaspoon salt

1–2 tablespoons water, if needed

STEAM THE TOFU over boiling water for 5 minutes. Turn onto a cotton towel to cool and pat dry. Crumble with a fork.

In a blender, combine the tofu, agave nectar or honey, carob powder, oil, nut butter, vanilla, and salt. Process until very smooth, stopping to scrape the sides of the container as needed. Add water as needed, but don't thin too much.

***Makes about 1 cup***
*(enough to frost a 9" layer cake or 13" × 9" cake)*

---

COOK'S TIP

✳ For a super birthday cake, bake a double recipe of Carob Fudge Cake (page 312) or Kamut-Maple Cake (page 315). Frost and pat finely chopped walnuts or pecans into the sides.

# Carob Fudge Glaze

*This easy glaze is soy-free and delicious.*
*A glaze is thin, so this doesn't make very much, just enough to glaze a cake.*

**2 tablespoons cashew, almond, or sunflower nut butter (smooth)**

**2 tablespoons carob powder, rubbed through a sieve**

**2–3 tablespoons light agave nectar or maple syrup**

IN A SMALL BOWL, combine the nut butter, carob powder, and 2 tablespoons of the agave nectar or maple syrup. Stir until smooth. If consistency is not thin enough, add the remaining 1 tablespoon agave nectar or maple syrup.

Spread the top of a cake, sending little trickles of glaze down the sides, without spreading the sides. Will even stretch to thinly cover a 13" × 9" cake.

*Makes about ½ cup*
*(enough to glaze an 8" or 9" layer cake or 13" × 9" cake)*

# Maple-Nut Frosting

*You can use this to decorate cakes.*

**8 ounces firm tofu, drained and cut into 1" cubes**

**¼ cup pecans or walnuts**

**Pinch of salt**

**1 tablespoon walnut oil**

**¼ cup maple syrup**

**Pecans or walnuts, chopped (optional)**

STEAM THE TOFU over boiling water for 5 minutes. Turn out onto a cotton towel to cool and pat dry. Crumble with a fork.

In a blender, combine the nuts and salt and process to a fine powder. Add the oil and process until very smooth. Pour in the maple syrup and process until blended.

Add half of the tofu, and process until smooth. With the blender running, add the remaining tofu, 1 chunk at a time, processing until very smooth after each addition, and stopping and scraping the sides of the container as necessary.

Chill at least 30 minutes. Spread over the cake and press chopped nuts if using into the frosting. Refrigerate until ready to serve.

*Makes about 1 cup*
*(enough to frost an 8" or 9" cake)*

---

### COOK'S TIPS

* For a super-smooth frosting, extract as much moisture as possible from the tofu before blending.

* To frost and fill a layer cake, double the recipe.

# Maple-Buttercream Frosting

*Sinfully sweet and a bit rich. I suggest you reserve this treasure*
*for special occasions. It's soy-free.*

8 ounces maple sugar

4–5 teaspoons hot water

1–2 tablespoons ghee (softened) or
Spectrum Spread

IN A BOWL, combine the maple sugar and 4 teaspoons of the water. Beat with electric beaters at low speed for about 1 minute, or until all of the sugar is moistened. Add another teaspoon of hot water if needed. Let mixture stand for 10 minutes.

Add the ghee or Spectrum Spread and beat for 3 minutes. Spread on cake or cookies.

*Makes about ¾ cup*
*(enough for the top and side of a layer cake or*
*13" × 9" cake)*

---

### COOK'S TIP

✳ To make ghee (clarified butter): Melt butter in a saucepan over low heat, then pour the liquid ghee into a jar, taking care to leave the milk solids in the bottom of the pan. Discard the solids. Ghee will keep frozen for up to 1 year.

# Maple Crème Topping

*This goat's-milk topping is very rich and sweet, like sweetened whipped cream, so it's best*
*reserved for birthdays or holiday desserts.*

¼ cup maple syrup

4 teaspoons ice water

½ cup powdered goat's milk

1 tablespoon lemon juice or ¼ teaspoon unbuffered vitamin C crystals

IN A DEEP BOWL, combine the maple syrup and water. Beat with electric beaters to combine. Sprinkle on half the milk powder, and beat on low speed. Gradually add the remaining milk powder, beating after each addition. Beat on high speed for 5 minutes. Add the lemon juice or vitamin C to taste. Chill. Spread over a cake.

*Makes ¾ cup*
*(enough for an 8" or 9" cake or a 13" × 9" cake)*

# Honey Glaze

*This makes a shiny thin glaze on cakes while adding a bit of moisture.*

¼ **cup honey**
¼ **cup fruit juice or water**

IN A SMALL SAUCEPAN, combine the honey and juice or water. Bring to a boil and cook for 4 to 5 minutes.

Prick the surface of a hot cake several times with a fork. Drizzle the glaze over the cake, spreading it to the edges.

*Makes ½ cup*
*(emough for an 8" or 9" cake)*

# Banana Topping

*This is a wonderful dairy-free topping for plain cakes and puddings.*
*It's also great on pancakes, waffles, and coffeecake-type breads.*

1 **large banana**
1 **tablespoon maple syrup**
   **Pinch unbuffered vitamin C crystals**

IN A SMALL BOWL, mash the banana and mix in the maple syrup and vitamin C. Using a fork, whip until the consistency of heavy cream.

For a topping, use as you would whipped cream.

*Makes about ½ cup*

---

COOK'S TIP

✳ If the tan color from the maple syrup bothers you, use light agave nectar instead.

# Carob-Nut Fudge Topping

*This sauce is rich, so use it sparingly. Good on plain cake or any ice cream.*

1⅓ cups warm water
¼ cup almond or cashew butter
½ cup honey
⅓ cup sifted carob powder
1 tablespoon almond oil
2 teaspoons vanilla extract

IN A BLENDER, combine the water and nut butter. Process for 2 or 3 seconds. With the blender running, add the honey, and process for 3 to 5 minutes, or until very smooth.

Pour into a 2-quart saucepan. Simmer, without stirring, for 5 minutes. Remove from the heat, and whisk in the carob, oil, and vanilla.

Use hot or cold. Keeps well for up to 2 weeks in a covered container in the refrigerator.

***Makes about 2 cups***

# Nutty Crème Topping

*This simple topping is free of dairy and soy. Make it ahead of time so it can chill and thicken in the refrigerator. For an attractive salt-and-pepper effect, use nuts that have a brown coating, like Brazil nuts or unblanched almonds. Use as you would whipped cream.*

½ cup cashews, almonds, or Brazil nuts
⅓ cup boiling water
2 tablespoons honey
½ teaspoon lemon juice or a pinch of unbuffered vitamin C crystals (optional)

IN A BLENDER, process the nuts to a fine powder. Add the water, honey, and lemon juice or vitamin C if using. Process on high speed for 2 minutes. Pour into a small bowl, and chill for 2 hours.

Store in a covered container in the refrigerator for up to 5 days.

***Makes 1 cup***

## Variations

*Maple-Almond Crème Topping:* Replace the honey and lemon juice or vitamin C with 2 tablespoons maple syrup and a few drops almond extract.

*Vanilla Crème Topping:* Replace the lemon juice or vitamin C with ¼ teaspoon vanilla extract.

# Whipped Tofu Topping

*Make in advance and chill. Use as you would whipped cream.*

8 ounces tofu, drained and cut into 1" cubes

2 tablespoons chopped raw cashews

2 tablespoons canola oil

2 tablespoons honey

1 teaspoon vanilla extract

2–4 tablespoons water

STEAM THE TOFU over boiling water for 5 minutes. Place on a cotton towel to cool and pat dry.

In a blender, process the cashews to a fine powder. Add the oil, honey, vanilla, and 2 tablespoons of the water. Process until well blended. Add tofu, a little at a time, until completely blended and creamy. If you desire a creamier consistency, blend in 1 to 2 tablespoons of the remaining water.

Cover and store in the refrigerator. Keeps for up to 4 days.

***Makes 1¼ cups***

# Apricot Topping

*Great over pancakes or over dessert.*

1 can (16 ounces) apricot halves packed in water or juice

2 tablespoons honey

1 tablespoon lemon juice or ¼ teaspoon unbuffered vitamin C crystals

DRAIN THE APRICOTS, reserving the juice for another use. Place in a blender and process for 10 to 15 seconds. Pour into a small saucepan. Add the honey and lemon juice or vitamin C. Bring to a boil over medium-high heat. Reduce heat and simmer for 5 minutes.

Serve warm or cold.

***Makes about 2 cups***

# Almond Dessert Sauce

*Use this over any plain cake, pudding, or fresh fruit as you would use cream.*

⅓ cup blanched whole almonds
1 tablespoon arrowroot
1 cup boiling water
¼ cup light agave nectar or honey
1 tablespoon almond oil
¼ teaspoon almond extract

IN A BLENDER, combine almonds and arrowroot and process until the almonds are powdered. Add the boiling water. Let stand 5 minutes. Add the agave nectar or honey and oil and process for 2 to 4 minutes, or until very smooth.

Pour into a small saucepan. Cook, stirring constantly, over medium heat for 2 minutes, or until thick and bubbly.

Remove from the heat and add the almond extract. Add more almond extract to taste.

Serve warm or cold.

*Makes 1¼ cups*

# Frosty Banana and Peach Sauce

*Serve in place of ice cream atop your favorite cake. Best when used while it's still thick and partially frozen, like a soft sherbet.*

1 cup chilled or partially frozen chopped peaches
1½ cups sliced frozen banana
2 teaspoons lemon juice or ⅛ teaspoon unbuffered vitamin C crystals
1–2 teaspoons light agave nectar or honey (optional)

PLACE THE PEACHES in the blender. Process for 10 to 15 seconds, or until pureed. With the blender running, add the banana slices, a few at a time, until all are incorporated and the mixture thickens to the consistency of soft ice cream. Add the lemon juice or vitamin C crystals. Add lemon juice, vitamin C, or agave nectar or honey to taste.

*Makes 2¼ cups*

## Variation

*Frosty Fruit Sauce:* Substitute strawberries, apricots, nectarines, cherries, or blueberries for the peaches.

---
### COOK'S TIP
---

* You can also make this sauce using frozen peaches (or other fruit) and unfrozen bananas. Just remember that one fruit must be frozen and one fruit must be a banana.

# Pineapple Glaze

*A quick glaze to jazz up plain cake.*

¼ cup thawed pineapple juice concentrate

2 tablespoons water

2 tablespoons light agave nectar or honey

IN A SMALL SAUCEPAN, combine juice concentrate, water, and agave or honey. Cook for 5 minutes, or until syrupy. Drizzle immediately over warm cake.

*Makes about ¼ cup (enough for 1 cake)*

# Pineapple Cake Filling

*A fruity, easy-to-make filling to sandwich between cake layers. Prepare this filling while the cake bakes, and allow it to cool to room temperature before spreading on a cooled cake.*

1 can (8 ounces) crushed pineapple, packed in juice

2 tablespoons arrowroot

1–2 tablespoons honey or maple syrup

⅛ teaspoon unbuffered vitamin C crystals

IN A BLENDER, combine the pineapple with juice, arrowroot, honey or maple syrup, and vitamin C and process for 1 minute. Pour into a small saucepan. Cook, stirring constantly, over medium heat for 3 minutes, or until thick and bubbly.

Remove from the heat, and allow to cool to room temperature.

*Makes 1 cup*

# Dessert Dip with Fruit

*Light and luscious, this easy, no-bake dish will satisfy your desire to end a meal on a sweet note.*

1½ cups goat's- or sheep's-milk yogurt

1–2 tablespoons light agave nectar or maple syrup

1–2 tablespoons minced fresh ginger

2–3 cups assorted chopped fresh fruit: strawberries, pineapple, bananas

A FEW HOURS OR A DAY AHEAD, combine the yogurt and agave nectar or maple syrup in a small bowl. Add 1 tablespoon of the ginger. Adjust the agave nectar or maple syrup and ginger to taste. Cover and refrigerate.

To serve, place a bowl of dip in the center of a plate. Arrange fruit around the bowl. Use toothpicks for dipping fruit pieces.

*Makes 1½ cups (about 4 servings)*

---

COOK'S TIPS

✳ Agave and maple syrup both mix with cold yogurt more easily than honey.

✳ Other chopped fresh fruit that works nicely in this recipe include grapes, apples, pears, peaches, and nectarines. Use singularly or in combination.

✳ You can slow the darkening of fresh fruit by tossing it with several tablespoons of orange or pineapple juice.

✳ If you have a garlic press, use it to crush the ginger.

### Variation

*Mint Dessert Dip with Fruit:* Replace the ginger with 6 to 8 fresh minced mint leaves. The mint flavor will develop more as the dip chills for a few hours, so right before serving, adjust the mint and agave nectar or maple syrup.

# Fudge Fondue for Fruit

*Another elegant—yet simple—dessert dip for fresh fruit. For chocolate lovers, this is a winner.*

- ¼ cup carob powder
- 1¼ teaspoons xanthan gum
- 1¼ cups whole goat's milk
- ⅓ cup light agave nectar or honey
- 1 tablespoon ghee or walnut or canola oil
- 1 teaspoon vanilla extract (optional)
- 2–3 cups assorted chopped fresh fruit: strawberries, pineapple, bananas

IN A 2-QUART SAUCEPAN, whisk together the carob and xanthan gum. Whisk in ½ cup of the goat's milk until smooth. Stir in the agave nectar or honey and remaining ¾ cup goat's milk and cook over medium-high heat for 5 minutes, or just until steaming (don't boil). Remove from the heat and stir in the ghee or oil and vanilla if using.

Serve warm, cold, or at room temperature.

To serve, place a bowl of fondue in the center of a plate. Arrange fruit around the bowl. Use toothpicks for dipping fruit pieces.

*Makes 4 servings*

---

COOK'S TIPS

✳ To make ghee (or clarified butter): Melt butter in a saucepan over low heat; then pour the liquid into a jar, taking care to leave the milk solids in the bottom of the pan. Discard the solids. Ghee will keep frozen for up to 1 year.

✳ You can slow the darkening of fresh fruit by tossing it with several tablespoons of orange or pineapple juice.

✳ To reheat the fondue, warm it over medium heat, stirring frequently.

✳ If the fondue should become lumpy, pour it into a blender and process briefly until thick and smooth, scraping the sides of the container as necessary.

✳ This fondue can also double as a hot fudge sauce for ice cream or cake.

# Holiday Foods

"T is the season to be jolly . . ." And people who have food allergies will feel lots jollier if holiday menus include foods they can eat freely, without risking an allergic reaction. Considering the emotional aspect of food at the holidays, that's especially important. Ask people about their family's holiday traditions and they'll start to tell you about special meals and mouthwatering menus they remember their parents and grandparents serving.

But, you may say, "There's too much to do to make two versions of everything!" You're right. The secret is to make delicious, satisfying "special" food that everyone can enjoy. That's what this section is all about. No one needs to know that the gravy is thickened with spelt, Kamut brand flour, or amaranth flour as long as it tastes terrific. If everyone raves about the fruit cake, what difference does it make whether it's held together with wheat flour or oat flour?

Many of the dishes featured here are also big hits at birthday parties, bridal showers, anniversaries, and other special events. When planning your festive meals, spend some time reviewing other chapters of this book for additional ideas, such as Meat, Poultry, and Game Dishes (page 213); Vegetable Sides and Salads (page 172); Salad Dressings, Sauces, and Condiments (page 190); Desserts (page 311); and Snacks (page 281). Most important, plan ahead with advance preparations so you can relax and enjoy yourself when guests arrive.

# Roast Pork

*Roast pork is a New Year's Day tradition, meant to ensure good luck, good health, and happiness in the year ahead. For people with food allergies, pork has additional allure as an alternative to beef and chicken. For people allergic to grains, pork is a rich source of vitamin $B_1$. Serve with sweet potatoes and Quick Applesauce (page 206).*

**1 pork leg or shoulder (about 5 pounds)**

PREHEAT THE OVEN to 325°F. Place the roast on a rack set in a pan. Cook, uncovered, for 35 minutes per pound, until cooked through and a meat thermometer registers at least 160°F. Remove from oven, and allow to stand for 15 minutes before carving.

*Serves about 10*

# Roast Lamb with Mint Sauce

*Lamb is most plentiful in the spring. That's part of the reason it's an Easter favorite. But lamb is a tasty alternative year-round for people who are allergic to beef or pork.*

**5–7 pounds lamb shoulder or leg**
**Mint Sauce (page 208)**

PREHEAT THE OVEN to 350°F. Remove the thin membrane covering the meat. Place the meat on a roasting rack, fat side up. Roast, uncovered, for 20 to 30 minutes per pound, or until the meat is cooked throughout and a meat thermometer registers at least 145°F. Allow roast to stand for 10 minutes before carving. Serve with the Mint Sauce.

*Serves 8 to 10*

---

### COOK'S TIP

* To use a meat thermometer, insert it in the thickest part of the meat, making sure it doesn't touch a bone. Insert a standard meat thermometer before starting to cook. Insert an instant-read variety near the end of the cooking time to check the meat's internal temperature, but don't expose this thermometer to oven heat or leave it in the meat for more than a minute.

# Sweet-Potato Casserole

*Make this side dish a day ahead to reduce the hassle of holiday meals.*

**4–6** large dark orange sweet potatoes
**1** can (20 ounces) crushed pineapple, packed in juice
**10–12** pecan halves (optional)

PREHEAT THE OVEN to 400°F. Oil a 13" × 9" baking dish. Pierce the potatoes in several places with the tip of a sharp knife. Place on baking sheets and bake for 1 hour, or until tender when tested with a fork. Allow to cool enough to handle. Remove the skins and place the flesh in a large bowl. Coarsely chop (or break up) and add the crushed pineapple with juice. Beat with an electric mixer until well blended and fluffy.

Spoon into the prepared baking dish and smooth the top. Arrange the pecans if using in an attractive pattern over potato mixture. Bake, uncovered, for 45 to 60 minutes, or until the potato mixture is bubbly and lightly brown around the edges.

*Serves 10 to 12*

---

### COOK'S TIPS

✳ To use a potato masher instead of an electric mixer: Drain the pineapple, reserving the juice. Mash the potatoes until smooth, adding the juice a little at a time. Stir in the crushed pineapple.

✳ If making the casserole ahead, cover and refrigerate it in the baking dish. Arrange the pecans on the top right before baking.

✳ If you cover this dish to keep it hot, be aware that the pecans will soften slightly.

# Stuffed Squash

*We love this at our house. It makes a hearty meatless meal at Thanksgiving.*

**1** large acorn squash, halved lengthwise and seeded
**1¼** cups water
**3** tablespoons walnut oil
**⅔** cup chopped onions
**1** apple, chopped
**1⅓** cups cooked chickpeas, soybeans, or pinto beans
**2** tablespoons lemon juice, 1 tablespoon vinegar, or

**¼** teaspoon unbuffered vitamin C crystals
**2** teaspoons thawed apple juice concentrate or maple syrup
**½** teaspoon salt
**¼** teaspoon ground cinnamon or freshly grated nutmeg
**⅓** cup chopped walnuts (optional)
**⅓** cup currants or raisins
**2** tablespoons sesame seeds (optional)

PREHEAT THE OVEN to 350°F. Place the squash, cut side down, in a baking dish and pour in 1 cup of the water. Bake for 30 to 40 minutes, or until tender when tested with a fork.

Heat the oil in a skillet over medium heat. Add the onions and apple and cook, stirring often, for 10 to 12 minutes, or just until the apples are tender. Do not overcook the apples. Remove from the heat.

In a food processor, combine the chickpeas, soybeans, or pinto beans; lemon juice, vinegar, or vitamin C crystals; juice concentrate or maple syrup; salt; cinnamon or nutmeg; and remaining ¼ cup water.

Process until well mixed. Add to the apple mixture and stir in the nuts if using and currants or raisins.

Spoon into the squash. Sprinkle with the sesame seeds if using. Bake for 20 to 30 minutes, or until heated through.

*Makes 4 servings*

# Spiced Fruit Compote

*This festive holiday treat doubles as a convenient side dish on busy nights.*
*To serve as a side dish, omit the agave nectar or honey.*

1 **cup prunes**

1 **cup dried apricots or peaches**

1 **cup quartered dried figs**

1 **cup raisins**

2 **cinnamon sticks**

¼ **teaspoon ground cloves or 3–4 whole cloves**

1–2 **tablespoons lemon juice or ¼ teaspoon vitamin C crystals**

2 **tablespoons light agave nectar or honey**

PLACE THE PRUNES, apricots or peaches, figs, raisins, cinnamon, and cloves in a 3-quart saucepan. Add enough water to cover the fruit. Bring to a boil, reduce the heat, and cook for 15 minutes. Cool slightly, discard the cinnamon sticks and whole cloves if using, and add the lemon juice or vitamin C crystals and agave nectar or honey. Serve warm or cold.

*Makes about 6 cups*

# Holiday Salad Mold

*A delicious, delicate pink salad for holiday buffets or potluck suppers.*
*Make this colorful dish a day ahead and you will love it even more.*

3 cups fresh cranberries (12 ounces)

1½ cups frozen pineapple juice concentrate, thawed (12 ounces)

1½ cups cool water

1 can (20 ounces) crushed pineapple, packed in juice

3 tablespoons or packages unflavored gelatin

2 tablespoons lemon or lime juice or ¼ teaspoon unbuffered vitamin C crystals

1½ cups halved seedless grapes

2 bananas, sliced

OIL A BUNDT PAN, 13" × 9" baking dish, or 3-quart mold.

In a 4-quart saucepan, combine 2 cups of the cranberries, the juice concentrate, crushed pineapple with juice, and ¾ cup water. Bring just to a boil. Reduce heat and cook, stirring occasionally, for 15 minutes.

In a small bowl, sprinkle the gelatin over the remaining ¾ cup water and allow to soften for 5 minutes.

Remove the cranberry mixture from the heat and add the gelatin mixture, stirring until the gelatin is dissolved and well blended. Stir in the lemon or lime juice or vitamin C crystals and refrigerate for about 1 hour, or just until the mixture has started to thicken.

Meanwhile, place the remaining 1 cup cranberries in a food processor and process until chopped. Add to the gelled mixture. Add the grapes and bananas. Stir gently to mix.

Pour into the prepared pan or mold. Cover with foil (but don't allow the foil to touch the salad) and chill 2 hours or until firm.

### Makes 16 servings

---

#### COOK'S TIPS

* If you've used a Bundt pan or decorative mold, unmold the salad on a bed of lettuce before serving. If you've used a 13" × 9" baking dish, cut the salad into squares.

* Optional ingredients that work very nicely in this salad include ½ cup chopped pecans or walnuts; 1 tart apple, chopped; and 1 pear, chopped. Use singularly or in combination.

# Nutty Pumpkin Pie with Honey

*A no-bake pumpkin pie that's free of eggs, soy, and cream. Perfect for any fall or winter festivities—Halloween, Thanksgiving, or anytime at all. Soon after the first edition of this cookbook appeared, a local bakery added a very similar pie to their line. It became so popular that they started freezing it, then selling and shipping it to neighboring states. Imagine my surprise when I bought one and found their list of ingredients matched this recipe.*

½ cup Brazil nuts or cashews
1¼ cups boiling water
1⅓ cups pumpkin puree
½ cup honey or agave nectar
½ teaspoon ground cinnamon
¼ teaspoon freshly grated nutmeg
¼ teaspoon powdered ginger
¼ teaspoon salt
⅛ teaspoon ground cloves
3 tablespoons arrowroot
2 tablespoons cool water
1 baked Spelt-Kamut Pie Crust
  (page 324)

IN A BLENDER, grind the nuts to a fine powder. With the motor off, scrape the bottom of jar with a spatula and blend again. Add ½ cup of the boiling water and process for 2 minutes. Add the remaining ¾ cup boiling water and blend for 10 to 20 seconds.

Add the pumpkin, honey or agave nectar, cinnamon, nutmeg, ginger, salt, and cloves. Blend well.

In a 3-quart saucepan, dissolve the arrowroot in the cool water. Stir in the pumpkin mixture. Bring to a boil, stirring often. Reduce the heat and cook for 3 minutes. Remove from the heat, let cool until lukewarm, and pour into the pie shell. Chill a few hours before serving.

***Makes 8 servings***

## Variations

*Nutty Pumpkin Pie with Molasses:* Replace half the honey with molasses or sorghum. Or try half dark and half light agave nectar.

*Nutty Pumpkin Pie with Nut Crust:* Replace the Spelt-Kamut Pie Crust with Nut and Seed Crunch Crust (page 327).

# Tofu Pumpkin Pie

*A dairy-free, egg-free version of a favorite holiday dessert.*

8 ounces firm tofu

1 Spelt-Kamut Pie Crust (page 324)
  or Rice-Flour Pie Crust (page 325)

⅓ cup vegetable oil

2 tablespoons lemon juice
  or ½ teaspoon unbuffered vitamin C
  crystals

1 tablespoon lecithin granules
  (optional)

½ teaspoon salt

½ cup honey or light agave nectar

2 tablespoons dark agave nectar

1 can pumpkin puree

1¼ teaspoons ground cinnamon

½ teaspoon powdered ginger

¼ teaspoon ground cloves

PREHEAT THE OVEN to 350°F. Drain the tofu for 20 to 30 minutes and press it between towels to extract as much moisture as possible. Crumble with a fork.

In a blender or food processor, combine the oil, lemon juice or vitamin C crystals, and salt. Add the tofu, half at a time, and process until smooth. With the processor running, add the honey or agave nectar in a thin stream. Add the pumpkin, cinnamon, ginger, and cloves. Process until smooth.

Pour into the pie crust, and bake for 50 to 55 minutes, or until the filling looks puffy and a knife comes out clean when inserted halfway between the center and the crust. The filling will set more as the pie cools.

***Makes 8 servings***

---

#### COOK'S TIP

✱ Instead of the dark agave nectar, you can use
  sorghum or molasses.

## Variation

*Crustless Pumpkin Pudding:* Omit the pie crust and pour the pumpkin mixture into an oiled baking dish. Cool before serving.

# Date Pecan Pie

*Although free of eggs and corn syrup, this tastes as good as traditional pecan pie.*
*And it's not as syrupy sweet as most other versions.*

½ **pound medjool dates, pitted and diced**

2 **cups water**

3 **tablespoons sorghum, molasses, or dark agave nectar**

1 **tablespoon unflavored gelatin**

1½ **teaspoons vanilla extract**

1 **baked Spelt-Kamut Pie Crust (page 324) or Rice-Flour Pie Crust (page 325)**

1 **cup pecan halves, toasted**

IN A SAUCEPAN, combine the dates and 1 cup of the water. Bring to a simmer and cook for 5 minutes. Cool for 5 to 10 minutes and place in a blender. Process until smooth. Add the sorghum, molasses, or dark agave nectar. Blend well, return to the saucepan, and keep warm over low heat.

In a small bowl, sprinkle the gelatin over the remaining 1 cup water. Allow to soften for 5 minutes. Add to the saucepan. Cook, stirring, over low heat for 2 minutes to dissolve the gelatin. Remove from the heat and let cool for 10 minutes.

Stir in the vanilla. Refrigerate for 20 to 30 minutes, or until thick and just starting to set. Pour into the pie shell. Arrange the pecans on top and press lightly. Chill for 2 hours before serving.

***Makes 8 servings***

---
### COOK'S TIP

✳ To roast large whole nuts, spread them on a baking sheet. Bake at 300°F for 12 minutes, or until light brown and fragrant.

## Variation

*Arrowroot Pecan Pie:* Omit the gelatin. Stir 4½ teaspoons arrowroot into the second cup of water. Add to date mixture in the saucepan. Bring to a boil and simmer for 3 minutes. Remove from the heat and let cool 10 minutes before adding the vanilla. Chill for about 15 minutes, or until cool to the touch. Pour into the pie shell and chill 4 hours or more before cutting.

# Plum Pudding

*This is one of the most traditional of all holiday desserts. (Any boiled or steamed pudding that contains fruit and spices is called a plum pudding, even if it doesn't contain plums.) Because this pudding is quite rich, you may want to start with small portions. Serve with Almond Dessert Sauce (page 347).*

2 cups unsweetened pineapple, apple, or white grape juice

½ pound dates, chopped

14 chopped dried figs, stems removed

⅓ cup honey or light agave nectar

⅓ cup molasses, sorghum, or dark agave nectar

⅓ cup canola oil

1 tablespoon grated lemon rind or ¼ teaspoon unbuffered vitamin C crystals

2¾ cups white buckwheat flour or 1½ cups white buckwheat flour + 1¼ cups quinoa flour or flakes

¼ cup arrowroot or tapioca starch flour

1 teaspoon ground cinnamon

1 teaspoon baking soda

½ teaspoon grated nutmeg

½ teaspoon powdered ginger

¼ teaspoon ground cloves

OIL A 2-QUART METAL MOLD or four 2-cup molds.

Pour the juice into a 3-quart saucepan. Add the dates and figs. Bring to a boil, reduce the heat, and simmer for 5 minutes. Remove from the heat and let cool. Add the honey or light agave nectar; molasses, sorghum, or dark agave nectar; oil; and lemon rind or vitamin C crystals. Stir well.

In a large bowl, whisk together the flours, cinnamon, baking soda, nutmeg, ginger, and cloves. Add the fruit mixture, stirring until well mixed. Pour into the prepared molds, filling them about three-quarters full. Cover the molds with waxed paper or foil and tie with string.

Place the mold (or molds) on a rack in a large stockpot. Add enough boiling water to the pot to come halfway up the sides of the mold. Cover and cook over medium heat for 3 hours. Do not remove the lid during the cooking time. Carefully remove the mold and place on a rack to cool.

Serve warm or allow to cool completely, wrap, and refrigerate until needed.

***Makes 16 servings***

---

### COOK'S TIPS

* Chopped prunes, raisins, and currants are also delicious in this pudding. Use singularly or in combination; you'll need about 3 cups total dried fruit.

* If you want, you can replace the buckwheat and quinoa flours with part brown rice flour and part oat flour or part spelt, part Kamut brand flours.

* To make white buckwheat flour, grind ½ cup white, unroasted whole groats at a time in a blender for 1 to 2 minutes. Pour into sieve. Repeat grinding, adding any groats that didn't go through the sieve.

* Need molds? Try using 1-pound coffee cans or 20-ounce cans from canned fruit.

* To remove the pudding from the mold, turn upside down and tap firmly on the counter.

* To reheat small portions, wrap a slice or two in paper towels or a cloth napkin and cook in a microwave oven for 30 seconds. Or place in a steamer basket over hot water. Cover with a tight-fitting lid and steam for 5 minutes, or until warm and moist (but not soggy).

## Variations

*Amaranth Plum Pudding:* Replace the quinoa with amaranth.

*Grain-Free Plum Pudding:* Omit the molasses or sorghum. If you don't have dark agave nectar, use $\frac{2}{3}$ cup honey.

# Pineapple-Cranberry Bread

*What a festive holiday bread! You can make it well in advance and freeze it.*

1⅓ cups white spelt flour

1⅓ cups Kamut brand flour

¼ cup date sugar

2 teaspoons baking soda

1 teaspoon xanthan gum

½ teaspoon salt

½ teaspoon grated nutmeg (optional)

½ cup chopped walnuts or almonds (optional)

1½ cups fresh cranberries or 1 cup dried

¼ cup thawed pineapple juice concentrate

1 cup unsweetened pineapple juice

½ cup drained crushed pineapple

¼ cup vegetable oil

2 tablespoons light agave nectar, honey, or water

PREHEAT OVEN to 400°F. Coat a nonstick 8½" × 4½" × 3" loaf pan with cooking spray.

Whisk together the spelt flour, Kamut brand flour, date sugar, baking soda, xanthan gum, salt, and nutmeg if using. Stir in the nuts if using and the cranberries.

In a blender or food processor, combine the pineapple juice concentrate; pineapple juice; crushed pineapple; oil; and agave nectar, honey, or water. Process for 2 minutes to completely liquefy the pineapple.

Add to the flour mixture, mixing just until the flour is moistened. Spoon into the prepared pan and immediately place in the oven. Reduce the heat to 325°F and bake for 40 minutes. Cover loosely with a foil "tent." Bake for 27 minutes more, or until cake tester inserted in the center comes out clean.

Cool in the pan on a rack for 15 to 20 minutes. Remove to the rack and cool completely.

***Makes 1 loaf***

### COOK'S TIPS

* To avoid keeping the oven door open for an extended time and losing oven heat, shape the foil tent before opening the door.

* When placing the cake on the rack, lay it on its side, perpendicular to the wires of the rack. The resulting marks can act as cutting guides so your slices will be of uniform thickness.

# Elegant and Easy Fruitcake

*This version of the traditional treat is so good that I made several to serve at a winter wedding.
Prepare the cake a few days ahead to allow flavors to "ripen."*

¾ cup unsweetened apple juice

¼ cup unsweetened pineapple juice

1 cup chopped dates

¾ cup chopped dried papaya
   or apricots

½ cup raisins or currants

¾ cup sifted brown rice flour

¾ cup sifted oat flour

1½ teaspoons baking soda

½ teaspoon ground cinnamon

¼ teaspoon grated nutmeg

2 large eggs, at room temperature

½ cup vegetable oil

1 cup chopped pecans or walnuts
   or ½ cup of each

   Pineapple Glaze (page 348) (optional)

PREHEAT THE OVEN to 325°F. Oil a 9" × 5" loaf pan. In a small saucepan, combine apple juice, pineapple juice, dates, papaya or apricots, and raisins or currants. Bring to a boil, remove from the heat, and cover the pan.

Into a large bowl, sift together the rice flour, oat flour, baking soda, cinnamon, and nutmeg. Whisk in the nuts.

In a small bowl, beat the eggs until well mixed. Slowly beat in the oil. Alternately, add the fruit mixture and the egg mixture to the flour mixture. Stir just until combined; do not overmix. The batter will be very thick.

Spoon into the prepared pan. Bake for 50 to 60 minutes, or until the cake is brown and a cake tester inserted in the center comes out clean.

Cool in the pan on a rack for 10 minutes. Remove to the rack, and if using the Pineapple Glaze, prick the top of the cake in 8 or 10 places and slowly drizzle the glaze over the cake.

Let cool completely. Wrap tightly in waxed paper or cellophane and overwrap with foil. Allow to ripen for a few days at room temperature; then refrigerate until needed.

***Makes 1 cake***

---

### COOK'S TIPS

✳ Because the cake is sticky, slice it with a wet serrated knife. (For easiest slicing, freeze cake for 2 hours before slicing; allow slices to return to room temperature before serving.)

✳ You can double this recipe; bake it in 2 loaf pans or 1 Bundt pan. If using the Bundt pan, bake for 70 to 75 minutes.

## Variation

*Grain-Free Fruitcake:* Replace the brown rice flour and oat flour with 1 cup sifted amaranth flour plus ½ cup arrowroot or tapioca starch flour; or use 1 cup white buckwheat flour and ½ cup of either amaranth or quinoa flour. (To make white buckwheat flour, grind ½ cup white, unroasted whole groats at a time in a blender for 1 to 2 minutes. Pour into a sieve. Repeat grinding, adding any groats that didn't go through the sieve.)

# Gingerbread Men

*Old-fashioned gingerbread cookies are especially fun to make for*
*Halloween, Thanksgiving, and Christmas.*

  2  **cups white buckwheat flour**
  ½  **cup date or maple sugar**
  1  **teaspoon baking soda**
1½  **teaspoons powdered ginger**
  ¼  **teaspoon unbuffered vitamin C**
     **crystals**
  ¼  **cup Spectrum Spread or vegetable oil**
  ¼  **cup molasses or dark agave nectar**
  2  **tablespoons water**
     **Currants, for eyes and buttons**
     **Dried papaya or mango, for mouths**
     **and noses**

PREHEAT THE OVEN to 350°F. Spray or
oil 2 sheets of 18"-long waxed paper. Oil the
bottom of a glass. Line 2 baking sheets with
parchment paper.

In a bowl, combine the flour, date or
maple sugar, baking soda, ginger, and vitamin C crystals. Make a well in the middle.

In a cup, combine the Spectrum Spread,
oil, molasses or dark agave nectar, and
water. Pour into the well in the flour mixture. Stir to blend. If mixture is too crumbly
to form into a ball, add more water, 1 tablespoon at a time.

Divide into 2 balls. Between the prepared
sheets of waxed paper, roll out each ball to
about ¼" thick. Carefully, remove the top
sheet and cut the dough with cookie cutters.
Using a wide spatula, place the cookies on
the prepared baking sheets. Reroll the trim-
mings until most are used. Gather the last
scraps, make one or two balls, and flatten
with the prepared glass to same thickness as
the Gingerbread Men.

Decorate the cookies by using currants
for eyes and buttons. Shape thin strips
of papaya into noses, mouths, collars,
and belts.

Bake for 8 to 10 minutes, or until the
cookies are firm and edges are just starting
to brown. Place the cookies, still on the
parchment, on a work surface to cool for 5
minutes. Carefully remove to a rack to cool
completely.

***Makes 10 to 15***

---

### COOK'S TIP

✻ To make white buckwheat flour, grind ½ cup white,
unroasted whole groats at a time in a blender for 1
to 2 minutes. Pour into a sieve. Repeat grinding,
adding any groats that didn't go through the sieve.

# Party Sponge Cake

*No one who has tasted this cake can believe it doesn't contain wheat.*
*It's as feather-light and airy as regular sponge cakes. Top it with a dessert sauce*
*or fill and frost. Perfect for birthday parties, wedding showers, and other special events.*

1 cup sifted maple sugar

1½ teaspoons grated lemon peel

¾ cup + 2 tablespoons potato starch
   or white buckwheat flour

1½ teaspoons Corn-Free Baking Powder
   (page 212)

6 egg yolks

¼ cup warm water

1 tablespoon lemon juice or 1 teaspoon
   vanilla extract

6 egg whites

½ teaspoon cream of tartar

Pineapple Cake Filling (page 348)
(optional)

Maple-Nut Frosting (page 342) or
Maple-Buttercream Frosting
(page 343) (optional)

PREHEAT THE OVEN to 350°F. In a small bowl, combine ¾ cup of maple sugar and the lemon peel.

Sift the potato starch, remaining ¼ cup maple sugar and the baking powder into another bowl. Sift again.

In a large bowl with an electric mixer set at medium speed, beat the egg yolks for 5 minutes, or until light colored and thick. Beat in the lemon-sugar mixture, sprinkling in ¼ cup at a time. Beat in the water and lemon juice or vanilla. The mixture should be very thick and fluffy. At low speed, beat in the flour mixture.

In another bowl, beat the egg whites at low speed until frothy. Beat in the cream of tartar. Change the speed to medium and beat for 1 minute. Increase speed to high and beat for about 2 to 2½ minutes, or until stiff, shiny peaks form. Don't beat until whites become dry.

Using a rubber spatula, gently fold the whites into the yolk mixture. Mix just until all traces of the egg whites disappear.

Pour into a 9½" angel-food cake pan with removable bottom. Bake for 35 to 40 minutes, or until the top is a deep golden brown and the cake springs back when lightly touched.

Let cool, upside down, in the pan on a rack for 1½ to 2 hours, or until completely cool. Remove from the pan and brush all loose crumbs from the top and sides.

If you want to fill the cake, use a serrated knife to cut the cake in half horizontally. Fill with the pineapple filling if using and reassemble. Frost the top and sides with the frosting, if using. Chill for about 30 minutes before serving.

***Makes 1 (about 10 servings)***

---

### COOK'S TIPS

∗ For best results when beating egg whites, be sure the bowl and beaters are clean and dry. Even a smidgen of fat can cause the whites to remain thin and watery. Eggs separate most easily when they're cold. Allow the separated yolks and whites to stand

15 to 20 minutes, covered, to warm to room temperature before beating.

✳ Invert the center tube of the cake pan over the neck of a sturdy bottle for cooling.

✳ To remove the cake from the pan, run a thin, sharp knife around the sides of the cake to loosen it. Press firmly on the bottom of the pan to lift the cake up out of the pan sides. Next, run the knife around the removable bottom and around the inside edges next to the tube. Gently invert the cake onto a serving plate.

✳ Here's a handy way to chop the lemon peel and sift the maple sugar at one time: Process the sugar in a food processor until it's reduced to a fine powder. Measure the 1 cup needed and return the rest to a storage container. Set aside the ¼ cup of maple sugar to sift with the flour. Return the ¾ cup back to the processor. Add about ten 2" strips of lemon peel and process for 1 to 2 minutes until finely ground.

✳ To make white buckwheat flour, grind ½ cup white, unroasted whole groats at a time in a blender for 1 to 2 minutes. Pour into a sieve. Repeat grinding, adding any groats that didn't go through the sieve.

✳ Don't substitute a Bundt cake pan for the 2-piece tube pan.

# Hidden Treasures

*There's no cooking involved in these easy-to-make treats, but they're elegant enough to present as a gift or to serve at holiday dinners or birthday parties. And they're easy enough to make that the kids can help.*

1 cup almond, cashew, or peanut butter, at room temperature

½ cup light agave nectar or honey

½ cup carob powder

½ cup shredded unsweetened coconut or toasted sesame seeds

60 raisins

20 toasted almonds

IN A BOWL, cream the nut butter and agave nectar or honey. Gradually mix in the carob. The mixture will be quite stiff and rather dry. Test the consistency by pinching a bit of dough between your fingers. It should mold well and hold its shape. If not, add water a teaspoon at a time.

Place the coconut or sesame seeds in a small bowl. Shape about a teaspoonful of dough around a small cluster of raisins (about 3) or 1 almond, covering the item completely. Roll in the coconut or sesame seeds. Repeat until all dough is used. Refrigerate for 1 hour before serving. Store in the refrigerator.

*Makes about 40*

### COOK'S TIP

✳ If you prefer all almond centers or all raisins, omit one and double the other.

# Carob-Nut Butter Fudge

*This is a rich confection, so cut it into small squares.*
*Most other fudge recipes use milk powder. This one doesn't.*

　1 cup almond, cashew, or peanut butter
　¼ cup light agave nectar or honey
　¼ cup carob powder
　¼ cup ground nuts (use same type as nut butter used)
　¼ cup chopped nuts (use same type as nut butter used)
　2 tablespoons toasted sesame seeds (optional)
12–16 raisins (optional)

IN A BOWL, combine the nut butter and agave nectar or honey. Stir in the carob, ground nuts, chopped nuts, and sesame seeds if using. The mixture will be very thick and stiff.

Press into an 8" × 4" loaf pan. Press the raisins if using onto the top. Chill. Cut into 1" squares.

***Makes 32 pieces***

---

### COOK'S TIP

＊ To toast small nuts and seeds, spread them in a small nonstick skillet. Cook, stirring often, over medium-low heat for 5 minutes, or until lightly browned and fragrant.

## Variation

*Coconut Fudge:* Replace the ground nuts with ¼ to ½ cup flaked unsweetened coconut. Sprinkle the top of fudge with additional coconut if desired and press into the top.

# Cranberry-Apple Cider Punch

*Rosy-colored and fragrant, this holiday punch is pleasantly sweet-tart. Serve it hot or make the concentrate ahead and serve as a cold punch.*

3 **cups cranberries (12 ounces)**

12 **ounces frozen apple juice concentrate, thawed**

12 **cloves, tied in cheesecloth or in a metal tea infuser**

4 **cinnamon sticks**

1 **gallon apple cider**

2 or 3 **small apples studded with cloves (optional)**

COMBINE THE CRANBERRIES, the juice concentrate, cloves, cinnamon, and 1½ cups of the cider in a 5-quart stainless-steel or enamel pot. Bring to a boil, reduce the heat, and simmer for 30 minutes. Cool for 10 minutes. Discard the cloves and cinnamon sticks.

Pour through a strainer into a large bowl, pressing the cranberries firmly with a spoon and scraping the pulp off the bottom with a spatula. Pour into a jar and chill for several hours.

To serve, combine the cranberry mixture and remaining 14½ cups chilled cider in a punch bowl. Add the apples if using.

***Makes about 1 gallon***
*(32 half-cup servings)*

---

### COOK'S TIPS

* In lieu of a sieve, you can press the cranberry mixture through a food mill. Use a rubber spatula to scrape the pulp off the bottom.

* Some tiny cranberry seeds may pass through the sieve. If this bothers you, line the sieve with a double layer of cheesecloth and strain it again. (I don't usually take this extra step.)

* If the punch will stand for a few hours, use some of the remaining cider to make ice cubes and add them when first assembling the punch.

## Variation

*Mulled Apple Cider:* Add all of the cider when cooking the cranberries. Discard the spices and strain. Add the apples, keep warm over low heat, and serve in mugs.

# Cranberry-Pineapple Punch

*A great apple-free alternative to apple cider.*

4 **cups cranberries (1 pound)**

⅔ **cup honey**

12 **cloves, tied in cheesecloth or in a metal tea infuser**

4 **cinnamon sticks**

2 **cans (46 ounces each) pineapple juice**

1 **quart ice water, chlorine- and fluoride-free**

1 **can (8 ounces) packed-in-juice pineapple rings (optional)**

IN A 5-QUART stainless-steel or enamel pot, combine the cranberries, honey, cloves, cinnamon, and 3 cups of the juice. Bring to a boil, reduce the heat, and cook for 30 minutes. Cool for 10 minutes. Discard the cloves and cinnamon sticks.

Pour through a strainer into a large bowl, pressing the cranberries firmly with a spoon and scraping the pulp off the bottom with a spatula. Pour into a jar and chill for several hours.

Drain the pineapple rings if using, reserving the juice. Add juice to the cranberry mixture and put the rings in a plastic bag and freeze them.

To serve, combine the cranberry mixture, iced water, and remaining 8½ cups pineapple juice in a punch bowl. Add the pineapple rings if using.

*Makes about 1 gallon*
*(32 half-cup servings)*

---

### COOK'S TIPS

＊ In lieu of a sieve, you can press the cranberry mixture through a food mill. Use a rubber spatula to scrape the pulp off the bottom.

＊ Some tiny cranberry seeds may pass through the sieve. If this bothers you, line a sieve with a double layer of cheesecloth and strain it again. (I don't usually take this extra step.)

＊ If the punch will stand for a few hours, use some of the remaining pineapple juice to make ice cubes and add them when first assembling the punch.

## Variation

*Mulled Cranberry-Pineapple Juice:* Add all of the juice and water when cooking the cranberries. Discard the spices and strain. Drain the pineapple rings, add pineapple packing juice to the cranberry mixture, and reserve the rings at room temperature. After chilling the cranberry mixture, add the pineapple rings, keep warm over low heat, and serve in mugs.

# Picnic, Camping, and Outdoor Foods

There's something special about eating outdoors. Everything seems to taste better in the open air.

You can adapt ideas for picnic menus from nearly every chapter of this book; you are sure to find suitable breads, pasta salads, crackers, cookies, burgers, and hot main dishes. Many recipes can be prepared at home, wrapped up, and enjoyed in the park.

The recipes I've gathered in this chapter include easy take-along foods as well as special mix-at-home, cook-in-camp dishes like Sunny Camp Cakes, Rice-and-Lentil Camp Supper, and Mung Bean Chowder. If you're out camping, don't forget beverages—see the Drinks, Milks, and Smoothies chapter on page 301 for making fruit concentrates. And remember to carry plenty of water with you.

If you're camping, check out Super Soups, Stews, and Chowders on page 135 too. One-pot meals are a natural when you're cooking over a campfire. Marjorie Fisher's

Venison Stew with Carrots (page 150), Rabbit-Vegetable Stew (page 149), and Catfish Chowder (page 155) are perfect. If you catch local fish, you can bake it, wrapped in foil, over the coals (as well as prepare it on the patio grill at home, of course). For more tips, see Baked Fish Fillets on page 236 and Broiled Fish on page 237. To make Glazed Puffed Amaranth (page 287) for a quick on-the-road snack, take along puffed amaranth and puffed quinoa, along with a little oil and agave nectar.

When I was a Girl Scout over 50 years ago, I learned the secret of a successful outing: Be prepared. It still holds true today. Make a list of the equipment and food you need to bring. Make your menus and prepare dry mixes in advance. If you want cookies and other baked goods, bake, package, and freeze well in advance. With a little practice, you will find you can stay on your special diet just as well outdoors as you can at home.

# No-Bake Granola

*This is a nice muesli-like breakfast food for campers to carry. Because it doesn't need honey or oil, this recipe is less sweet and rich than traditional granolas, but it still captures that characteristic flavor and crunch. I like to use the less-common nuts like Brazil nuts, filberts, macadamias, and pine nuts.*

½ cup sunflower seeds

½ teaspoon salt

2 cups quick-cooking oats

1 cup chopped Brazil nuts, filberts, or macadamias

½ cup grated unsweetened coconut

½ cup chopped dried unsweetened pineapple

½ cup chopped dried papaya

Pineapple Milk (page 305), juice, or herbal tea

IN A BLENDER or food processor, combine the sunflower seeds, salt, and 1 cup of the oats. Process until finely ground. Place in a large bowl. Add the remaining oats, nuts, coconut, pineapple, and papaya. Toss to combine. Store in zip-close plastic bags, in the refrigerator.

Serve moistened with pineapple milk, juice, or herbal tea.

***Makes 8 servings***

---

### COOK'S TIPS

* If you want, replace the pineapple and papaya with your choice of dates, raisins, currants, and prunes or dried apricots, peaches, and apples.

* When you're on the Rotary Diversified Diet and limiting the number of food families, choose either sunflower seeds or nuts—but not both.

* To prepare the granola at a campsite: Omit the grinding step to produce a delightfully chewy granola. To serve, moisten with fruit juice or herb tea and allow to soak for 5 minutes.

# Trail Mix

*Don't reserve this just for backpacking. It's a wonderful snack any time. You can vary the ingredients to suit your personal taste. Use either raw or toasted nuts.*

1 cup raisins

1 cup chopped dried pineapple or apricots

1 cup whole cashews

1 cup almonds

1 cup walnuts or pecans or ½ cup each

½ cup sunflower seeds

½ cup pumpkin seeds

IN A LARGE BOWL, combine the raisins, pineapple or apricots, cashews, almonds, walnuts or pecans, sunflower seeds, and pumpkin seeds. Mix and store in tightly covered jars in the refrigerator.

***Makes 6 cups***

---

### COOK'S TIPS

\* To toast small nuts and seeds, spread them in a small nonstick skillet. Cook, stirring often, over medium-low heat for 5 minutes, or until lightly browned and fragrant.

\* To roast large whole nuts, spread them on a baking sheet. Bake at 300°F for 12 minutes, or until light brown and fragrant.

\* To personalize your mix, you can replace any of the nuts with Brazil nuts, macadamia nuts, filberts, or pine nuts. You can vary the seeds, too, but note that very small ones, like sesame, settle to the bottom and can be difficult to eat.

\* If you're on a Rotary Diversified Diet, you might want to improvise your own Trail Mix using fewer food families. You can also put together 4 different combinations of fruits and nuts for a custom-made mix for each of the 4 days.

# Carrot Survival Bars

*These are not a cookie or a casual snack food. They're designed so that just two bars, plus a little fresh or dried fruit, supply all the nutrients needed for a single meal. My guess is that they are adequate in all of the essential nutrients except vitamin D. And if you're out hiking or swimming, you're getting your quota of that vitamin from the sun. Make them at home to carry with you; they'll keep without refrigeration for 5 to 7 days.*

2 cups finely chopped carrots, lightly packed (about 13 ounces)

1 cup rolled oats

¾ cup amaranth or quinoa flour

½ cup oat bran

¼ cup powdered goat's milk

⅓ cup sunflower seeds

2 tablespoons sesame or hemp seeds (optional)

1 teaspoon anise seeds

¾ teaspoon salt

2 tablespoons light or dark agave nectar, honey, or sorghum

¼ cup canola oil

1 jar (4 ounces) baby food green peas

IN A BOWL, combine the carrots, rolled oats, amaranth or quinoa flour, oat bran, goat's milk, sunflower seeds, sesame or hemp seeds if using, anise, and salt. Toss to mix.

Heat the agave nectar, honey, or sorghum in a small saucepan until it lique-fies. Remove from the heat and stir in the oil and peas. Stir into the carrot mixture. Mixture will be stiff. Allow to rest for 10 to 15 minutes.

Meanwhile, preheat the oven to 350°F. Line a baking sheet with parchment.

Using a large spoon, drop the carrot mix-ture into 8 mounds on the baking sheet. Using a spatula, shape each mound into a small log about the size of a hot dog. Bake for 20 minutes. Turn the logs over, and bake for 20 minutes more.

Remove to racks to cool. Store in a tightly covered container for use within a few days. Or wrap and freeze. Bars will keep 5 to 7 days at room temperature or for up to 3 months in the freezer.

***Makes 8***

---

### COOK'S TIPS

✳ To chop the carrots in a food processor, use the steel blade, not the grating disk.

✳ If you don't have a food processor, you may wish to grate the carrots.

## Variations

*Carrot Bars with Buckwheat:* Replace the ama-ranth flour with buckwheat flour.

*Carrot Bars with Nuts:* Add ¾ cup chopped hazelnuts or other nuts to the carrot mix-ture, either in addition to the seeds or to re-place them.

# Fig Fudge

*Dried fruits and seeds are concentrated sources of nutrients and energy,
so they're perfect trail food. Make this fudge at home a day or so before your outing.
It keeps well and packs easily.*

¼ cup toasted sunflower seeds

1 cup chopped dates

8–10 large figs, chopped (discard stem ends)

¼ teaspoon unbuffered vitamin C crystals

2 tablespoons toasted sunflower seeds (optional)

PLACE THE SUNFLOWER seeds in a food processor, and process briefly. Add the dates, figs, and vitamin C. Process until well chopped and mixture forms a ball atop the metal blade. Press into a loaf pan or mess kit. Press the 2 tablespoons of sunflower seeds into the top if using. Chill until needed.

***Makes ¾ pound***

---

#### COOK'S TIPS

✻ To toast small nuts and seeds, spread them in a small nonstick skillet. Cook, stirring often, over medium-low heat for 5 minutes, or until lightly browned and fragrant.

✻ If you've pressed the fudge into a loaf pan, cut into pieces, wrap, and freeze until you're ready to leave.

## Variation

*Sesame Fig Fudge Logs:* Form the fudge into a log shape. Roll it in ½ cup or more sesame seeds, pressing the seeds into the fudge.

# Rice-and-Lentil Camp Supper

*Made in one pot, this is a less-expensive, homemade version of the dehydrated meals sold in camp-supply stores. Very easy and nutritious, too. It may turn out to be your favorite camp-out meal.*

**DRY MIX**

- 1 cup brown rice
- ½ cup green or brown lentils
- 2 tablespoons dehydrated onion flakes
- 2 cloves
- ¾ teaspoon salt
- 1 bay leaf
- 1 tablespoon Savory Seed Seasoning (page 209)
- ½ teaspoon ground cinnamon
- ½ teaspoon powdered ginger
- ½ teaspoon ground cardamom
- ¼ teaspoon garlic powder
- Pinch of cayenne pepper (optional)

**LIQUIDS**

- 3½ cups water
- 3 tablespoons olive oil

TO MAKE THE DRY MIX: Combine the rice, lentils, onion flakes, cloves, salt, and bay leaf in a zip-close plastic bag. Combine the Savory Seed Seasoning, cinnamon, ginger, cardamom, garlic powder, and cayenne if using in another plastic bag.

Label the packages and make a notation to add oil and water.

*To prepare with the liquids:* Warm the oil in a large skillet or pot. Add the Savory Seed Seasoning mixture and cook for 10 minutes over low to moderate heat (less time if fire is very hot), stirring often. Don't let the seasonings burn.

In a small bowl or pot, rinse the rice and lentils with cold water. Drain through a sieve. Add to the seasoning mixture, stirring for 1 minute to coat the rice and beans. Add the water, cover, and bring to a boil. Cook for 45 minutes, or until rice and lentils are tender. Discard the bay leaf before serving.

***Makes 4 servings***

---

### COOK'S TIP

\* Don't use red lentils in this dish. They cook too quickly, before the rice is tender.

## Variation

*Curried Rice and Lentil Supper:* Replace the cinnamon, ginger, and cardamom with 2 to 3 teaspoons Curry Powder (page 211). For a highly seasoned dish, add the curry along with the other seasonings.

# Mung-Bean Chowder

*Pack this at home and take it on camp outings for a quickly prepared,*
*satisfying on-site soup. Mung beans are small and convenient to use*
*in camp because they don't need soaking.*

### DRY MIX

- 1 cup mung beans
- ¾ cup brown rice
- 1 tablespoon dehydrated onion flakes
- ¾ teaspoon salt
- 1 tablespoon Pizzazz Seasoning (page 210)
- 1 tablespoon Savory Seed Seasoning (page 209)
- ¼ teaspoon garlic powder

### VEGETABLES

- 5 cups water
- 2 cups chopped fresh vegetables: carrots and celery

TO MAKE THE DRY MIX: Combine the mung beans, rice, onion flakes, salt, Pizzazz Seasoning, Savory Seed Seasoning, and garlic powder in a zip-close plastic bag. Label and note to add water when ready to cook.

*To prepare with the vegetables:* Mix the mung-bean mixture and water. Bring to a boil, and cook, stirring occasionally, for 45 to 60 minutes. Add the vegetables 30 minutes before the end of the cooking time.

***Makes 4 servings***

---

### COOK'S TIPS

✳ Other vegetables you might use include turnips, peas, and cabbage. Use singularly or in combination.

✳ This soup can also be made without vegetables if you prefer.

## Variations

*Caraway Mung-Bean Chowder:* Replace the Pizzazz Seasoning with 1 teaspoon parsley flakes, ½ teaspoon ground cumin, ½ teaspoon dried dill weed, ½ teaspoon ground fennel, ¼ teaspoon ground caraway seeds, and ¼ teaspoon celery seeds.

*Lemon Mung-Bean Chowder:* Replace the Savory Seed Seasoning with 1 teaspoon lemon peel.

*Mung-Bean Chowder with Meat:* Add 1 cup cooked, chopped meat (or poultry or canned fish) to the chowder. (Or the fish can be freshly caught and cleaned.)

# Door County Fish Boil

*The culinary specialty of Door County, Wisconsin, is the fish boil, and it's a real treat. Locals cook up big pots of the fragrant stock over back-yard grills and fireplaces. They borrow long tables from churches and fire houses to set up in the shade. Recipes vary widely, with everyone having an opinion on which seasonings are best and whether or not to add onions, carrots, and potatoes to the pot. I favor including the vegetables to simplify preparation. Although an authentic fish boil is served with melted butter, the simple dill sauce given here makes an excellent substitute. This recipe serves four, but you can easily multiply it for a crowd.*

### FISH AND VEGETABLES

- 1½ quarts water
- 1 small onion, quartered
- ½ cup celery leaves or celery stalks, cut into ½" slices
- 1 tablespoon cider vinegar or lemon juice
- 1–2 bay leaves
- 1 teaspoon dried tarragon or dried dillweed
- ¼ teaspoon crushed fennel seeds
- 12 small new potatoes
- 6 carrots, cut into 3" pieces
- 1½ pounds whitefish fillets, divided into 4 pieces

### SAUCE

- 2 tablespoons rolled oats
- 4½ teaspoons dried dill weed
- 1 tablespoon mild Hungarian paprika
- ½ teaspoon salt
- 2 tablespoons ghee, melted, or vegetable oil
- 2–3 tablespoons finely chopped fresh parsley
- Lemon wedges (optional)

TO COOK THE FISH AND VEGETA-BLES: Combine the water, onion, celery, vinegar or lemon juice, bay leaf, tarragon or dill, and fennel in a Dutch oven or stockpot. (The pot should not be more than half full.) Bring to a boil. Reduce the heat, cover, and cook for 30 minutes.

Add the potatoes and carrots, and cook for 15 minutes.

Wrap 2 pieces of the fish in a square of cheesecloth, tying knots with opposite corners. Repeat with the remaining 2 pieces. Add to the vegetable mixture. When the mixture returns to a boil, reduce the heat, and cook for 10 minutes.

Remove the fish and vegetables to a warm platter. Discard the bay leaves before serving. Cover with foil to keep warm while preparing the sauce.

*To make the sauce:* Bring the cooking liquid to a boil, and cook for 5 to 10 minutes to reduce to 2 cups. Strain into a 2-cup measuring cup.

Combine the oats, dill, paprika, and salt

---

in a blender. Process until ground to a fine powder. Add the ghee or oil and cooking liquid. Process for 30 seconds. Pour into a small saucepan. Bring to a boil, stirring constantly. Add more paprika and salt to taste.

Serve the fish and vegetables topped with the sauce and parsley. Serve with the lemon if using.

*Makes 4 servings*

---

### COOK'S TIPS

* If you want, you can substitute ¼ to ½ teaspoon unbuffered vitamin C crystals for the vinegar or lemon juice.

* If you don't have small new potatoes, use 4 large red potatoes, quartered.

* For a more authentic fish boil, use a 2-pound whole, cleaned lake whitefish. Allow 15 minutes cooking time.

* If you will be serving a large crowd, you can prepare the sauce ahead. I occasionally cook a smaller version of the fish boil a week or two ahead of time so I can use that stock to make as much sauce as I'll need for the party. Then I prepare the sauce and freeze it until needed. It's a simple matter to reheat the sauce while the fish cooks. And it ensures that the piping-hot fish and vegetables will be served promptly to hungry guests.

* To make ghee (clarified butter): Melt butter in a saucepan over low heat; then pour the liquid ghee into a jar, leaving the milk solids in the bottom of the pan. Discard the solids. Ghee will keep frozen for up to 1 year.

## Variation

*Fish Boil with Monkfish:* Replace the whitefish with 1¾ pounds of monkfish.

# Sunny Camp Cakes

*These pancakes are specifically designed for campers. Mix the dry ingredients at home, then add the liquids when you're ready to cook. The powdered goat's milk increases the protein in the pancakes and improves their texture, too. Serve your cakes with maple syrup, fruit butter, or store-bought all-fruit preserves.*

## DRY MIX (ABOUT 7 CUPS)

- 4 cups **Kamut brand or rye flour**
- 1⅓ cups **amaranth or quinoa flour**
- 1 cup **powdered goat's milk (optional)**
- ½–¾ cup **sunflower seeds**
- 6 teaspoons **Corn-Free Baking Powder (page 212)**
- 2 teaspoons **salt**

## PANCAKES (2 SERVINGS)

- 1¾ cups **Dry Mix**
- 1 cup **water**
- 2 tablespoons **vegetable oil**
- 1–2 teaspoons **agave nectar or maple syrup**

TO MAKE THE DRY MIX: Combine the Kamut or rye flour, amaranth or quinoa flour, powdered milk if using, sunflower seeds, baking powder, and salt. Mix well. Package in zip-close plastic bags and label.

*To make the pancakes:* Preheat a griddle or a large nonstick skillet.

When griddle is hot, add the water, oil and agave or maple syrup to the dry mix, and stir just until combined.

Drop batter, 2 tablespoonfuls per cake, onto the griddle. Cook for 3 minutes, or until bubbly on top and brown on the bottom. Turn and cook for 2 to 3 minutes more.

*Makes 10, 6-inch cakes*

---

### COOK'S TIP

✳ Package the pancake mix according to your needs: For example, use four 1-pint freezer bags to hold 1¾ cups dry mix in each to serve two. Or use two 1-quart bags to hold 3½ cups dry mix in each to serve 4.

## Variations

*Buckwheat Sunny Camp Cakes:* Replace the Kamut brand or rye and amaranth or quinoa flours with 6 cups white buckwheat flour instead. (To make white buckwheat flour, grind ½ cup white, unroasted whole groats at a time in a blender for 1 to 2 minutes. Pour into sieve. Repeat grinding, adding any groats that didn't go through the sieve.)

*Grain-Free Sunny Camp Cakes:* Replace the Kamut brand or rye flour with 2 cups each of amaranth, white buckwheat, and quinoa flours. (See above for procedure for making white buckwheat flour.)

# BBQ Chicken

*Because this chicken is cooked indoors and then carried out to the picnic table to serve,
it's a great picnic alternative for people who are allergic to the fumes from gas or charcoal cookers.
Commercial barbecue sauces may contain sodium benzoate, cornstarch, corn syrup, hickory
smoke flavor, caramel color and unspecified spices and flavorings. If any of those ingredients
are a problem for you, try this quick and easy recipe.*

3–4 **pounds whole frying chicken, cut-up,
or skinless, boneless thighs, legs, and
breast halves**

¼ **cup honey- or fruit juice-sweetened
ketchup**

2 **tablespoons lemon juice
or ½ teaspoon unbuffered vitamin C
crystals**

2 **tablespoons dark agave nectar,
sorghum, or honey**

1 **teaspoon Dijon-style mustard**

¼ **teaspoon salt (optional)**

2 **tablespoons sesame seeds**

PREHEAT THE OVEN to 400°F. Remove
the skin from all pieces except the wings.
Arrange chicken in a single layer in a
baking dish.

In a small saucepan, combine the
ketchup, lemon juice or vitamin C, sweetener, mustard, and salt if using. Cook for 5
to 10 minutes. Brush the sauce over the
chicken. Sprinkle with the sesame seeds.

Bake the bone-in chicken for 35 to 45
minutes and boneless chicken for 30 minutes, or until the chicken is tender, no
longer pink, and a meat thermometer registers at least 180°F.

***Makes 4 servings***

---

### COOK'S TIP

✳ You can double or triple this recipe to serve a
crowd.

✳ If tomato is a problem for you, omit the commercial
ketchup and use Plum Ketchup (page 202).

# BBQ Baked Beans

*Commercially prepared baked beans can be a problem for people with allergies because they often contain sugar and corn syrup, plus ambiguous ingredients such as modified food starch and "natural flavoring." Slowly baking these beans contributes to their wonderful flavor and aroma.*

2 tablespoons olive oil

1½ cups chopped onions or leeks

⅔ cup chopped celery

⅔ cup chopped green bell peppers

2 cloves garlic, crushed

1 can (6 ounces) tomato paste

1 cup water, vegetable stock, or broth

¼ cup dark agave nectar or sorghum

¼ cup cider vinegar

1 teaspoon salt

2 tablespoons Dijon mustard

Dash of hot-pepper sauce or ⅛ teaspoon ground red pepper (optional)

4–4½ cups cooked unseasoned navy or Great Northern beans, rinsed and drained

PREHEAT THE OVEN to 300°F. Oil a 2½- or 3-quart baking dish (or a 13" × 9" baking dish).

Warm the oil in a large skillet or 3-quart saucepan over medium heat. Add the onions or leeks, celery, peppers, and garlic and cook for 7 minutes, or until soft. Stir in the tomato paste; water, stock, or broth; agave nectar or sorghum; vinegar; salt; mustard; and pepper sauce or ground red pepper if using. Cover and cook for 10 to 20 minutes. Stir in the beans and bring to a boil.

Pour into the prepared dish. Bake, uncovered, for 2½ hours. After one hour, check every 30 minutes for moisture and stir in ½ cup water as needed.

***Makes 6 servings***

---

### COOK'S TIPS

✳ If you want, you can substitute 1 can chopped green chiles for the green bell peppers. Add along with the stock or broth.

✳ Maple syrup is another sweetener that works well in this recipe.

✳ For picnics and back-yard barbecues, you can keep the beans warm for up to 2 hours by covering the dish and wrapping it in a beach towel.

✳ If vinegar bothers you, add ½ to 1 teaspoon unbuffered vitamin C crystals for tang.

✳ To cook dry beans: Soak 1⅔ cups dry navy or pea beans for 5 to 8 hours. Discard the soak water, cover with fresh water, about 1" above the beans. Cover and cook for 1 hour or until the beans are tender.

✳ To cook in a slow cooker: Double the recipe. Place the beans and the broth mixture in a 3½- or 4-quart slow cooker. Cover and cook on high for 1 hour. Reduce the heat to low and cook for 5 to 8 hours. Remove the lid only once, about 1 hour before they should be done. Stir the beans, re-cover, and finish cooking.

# Resources for Foods, Supplies, and Information

Many foods and household products made for people with allergies are available in health food stores, natural product shops, and even discount stores. For instance, lactose-free soy milk can be found in almost every health food store and many grocery stores. Water filters and air filters are available in Wal-Mart and Costco. And wheat-free pastas are on the shelves of most health food stores and supermarkets. However, some items are hard to track down. Here's a guide to hard-to-find foods, kitchen aids, and allergy-information services. This directory is by no means an all-inclusive list, nor does it constitute endorsement of any product or service by the author or publisher. However, we feel that the information will help you make the most of this cookbook.

To locate a food you're not familiar with, start in your health food store or large supermarket. Often they are delighted to special-order an item to meet their customer's needs. Or contact one of the sources listed below. Many have toll-free phone numbers and/or Web sites for ordering. The only additional cost to you will be shipping and handling charges. If you value your time and energy—and appreciate the lack of "hassle" that telephone ordering offers—you may decide (as I have) that the convenience of having products delivered to your door is well worth any additional cost.

If you don't find what you're looking for in the list below, try the Internet. It is an extremely useful source for tracking down non-allergenic foods and products.

## ALLERGY SAFETY MEASURES

### Health Enterprises, Inc.

90 George Leven Drive
North Attleboro, MA 02760
(800) 633-4243

Identification bracelets and necklaces listing allergies or other medical problems; medical-alert cards for wallets; medical-alert information kit for the home.

### MedicAlert Foundation

2323 Colorado Avenue
Turlock, CA 95382
(800) 432-5378
Web site: www.medicalert.com

The nation's leading emergency medical information service; provides bracelet or necklace listing allergies, medical conditions, and a hotline number to a central computerized data center. $35 fee to join. Since 1994 there is a $15 annual fee. You can update your medical information when you renew.

**Protectube™ Manufacturing Inc.**

9325 Yonge Street, Suite 152
Richmond Hill, Ontario
Canada L4C 0A8
(905) 760-9313
Web site: www.protectube.com

Protectube™ is a safe, convenient and inexpensive protective container for the Epipen®, the over-the-counter auto-injector that treats allergy and anaphylaxis.

## ASSOCIATIONS AND ALLERGY INFORMATION

**Allergy Adapt, Inc.**

1877 Polk Ave.
Louisville, CO 80027
(303) 666-8253
Web site: www.food-allergy.org

Publishes healthy, allergy-oriented recipe books, specializing in bread machine recipes and recipes for special and rotation diets.

**American Academy of Allergy, Asthma and Immunology**

611 E. Wells Street
Milwaukee, WI 53202
(800) 822-2762
Web site: www.aaaai.org

Largest professional medical specialty organization in the United States, representing allergists, asthma specialists, clinical immunologists, and others with a special interest in the research and treatment of allergic diseases. AAAAI serves as an advocate for the public by providing up-to-date educational information.

**American Academy of Environmental Medicine**

7701 E. Kellogg, Suite 625
Wichita, KS 67207-1705
(316) 684-5500
Web site: www.aaem.com

Physicians who treat allergies within the context of environmentally oriented medicine. Write or phone the AAEM office for names of members in your area.

**American Environmental Health Foundation, Inc.**

8345 Walnut Hill Lane, Suite 225
Dallas, TX 75231
(214) 361-9515
Web site: www.aehf.com

Nonprofit organization founded in 1975 to provide research and education into environmental illness. The AEHF store carries more than 1,800 environmentally safe, less- and non-toxic products for home, office, and school.

**American Celiac Society Dietary Support Coalition**

Ms. Annette Bentley
59 Crystal Avenue
West Orange, NJ 07052-3570
(973) 325-8837

Provides information about celiac disease.

**Asthma and Allergy Foundation of America**

1233 20th Street, NW, Suite 402
Washington, DC 20036
(800) 7-ASTHMA (800-727-8462)
Web site: www.aafa.org

Information about support groups; chapters and patient education (food allergy, childhood asthma, allergic rhinitis, asthma in the elderly, and the adverse effects of medications).

### Feingold® Association of the United States

127 E. Main Street, Suite 106
Riverhead, NY 11901
(800) 321-3287
Web site: www.feingold.org

Helps families of children with behavior and/or learning problems (ADD, ADHD) to avoid some synthetic food additives and natural salicylates; also helps chemically sensitive adults.

### Food Allergy Network

10400 Eaton Place, Suite 107
Fairfax, VA 22030-2208
(800) 929-4040
e-mail: fan@foodallergy.org
Web site: www.foodallergy.org

Mission is to increase public awareness about food allergies and anaphylaxis, to provide education, and to advance research on behalf of all those with food allergies.

### Gluten Intolerance Group

15110 10th Avenue SW, Suite A
Seattle, WA 98166
(206) 246-6652
Web site: www.gluten.net

Provides information on gluten intolerance and various services to adults and children. This includes the following for children: a camp, educational information, and parent support. Also has an annual education conference, quarterly newsletter, and videos.

### Healthy House Institute

430 N. Sewell Road
Bloomington, IN 47408
(812) 332-5073
Web site: www.hhinst.com

Publisher of books and videos on buildings and maintaining a healthy lifestyle.

### Human Ecology Action League, Inc. (HEAL)

P.O. Box 29629
Atlanta, GA 30359-0629
(404) 248-1898
Web site: http://members.aol.com/HEALNatnl/index.html (Web site address is case sensitive)
e-mail: HEALNatnl@aol.com

Provides services for those whose health has been adversely affected by environmental exposure (chemical susceptibilities, environmental or ecological illness, total allergy syndrome, twentieth-century illness).

### Mast Enterprises, Inc.

8800 N. Half Mile Lane
Hayden, ID 83835
(208) 772-8213
e-mail: mastent@nidlink.com
Web site: www.nidlink.com/~mastent

M. H. Jones (author of this book) is the former publisher of *Mastering Food Allergies,* a monthly newsletter that focused on new information about less common foods and how to use them, including recipes. Write or phone for back issues.

## HOUSEHOLD GOODS AND CLEANING PRODUCTS

### AFM Enterprises, Inc.

3251 Third Ave.
San Diego, CA 92103
(619) 239-0321

Supplies low-odor and nontoxic building and maintenance products that can be safely used by the chemically sensitive customer.

## Allergy Relief Shop

3360 Andersonville Highway
Andersonville, TN 37705
Order Line: (800) 626-2810
Consultation Line: (423) 494-4100
Web site: www.allergyreliefshop.com

Storefront, mail order, consulting, and construction company specializing in creating a safe environment for people who have allergies and/or are chemically sensitive. Catalog carries products ranging from health and beauty aids to paint sealers and dehumidifiers.

## Allergy Resources

301 E. 57th Avenue, Suite D
Denver, CO 80216
(800) 873-3529

40-page catalog. Hypoallergenic laundry and dishwashing products; carpet cleaner; natural foods; gluten-free flours; baking ingredients such as xanthan gum, agar powder, and arrowroot; alternative sweeteners such as white stevia powder; hypoallergenic bedding and pillows; air purifiers.

## L. Foust Co., Inc.

P.O. Box 105
Elmhurst, IL 60126
(800) EL-FOUST (800-353-6878)
Web site: www.foustco.com

Manufacturers of room air purifiers especially for people with chemical sensitivities.

## Janice Corp.

198 U.S. Highway 46
Budd Lake, NJ 07828
(800) JANICES (800-526-4237)
e-mail: jswack@worldnet.att.net

Dedicated to providing safe, healthy, natural fiber products. From bedding to socks, Janice is known as the "Natural Mail Order Department Store." Complete collection of bed, bath, kitchen, and personal items. When appropriate items cannot be found, Janice manufactures them in her own sewing room.

## Kiss My Face

P.O. Box 224
Gardiner, NY 12525
(800) 262-KISS

All natural body care company specializing in liquid soaps, moisturizers, and body oils. All products contain no artificial colors or unnecessary chemical additives and have not been tested on animals.

## Nature's Gate
## Levlad, Inc.

9200 Mason Avenue
Chatsworth, CA 91311
(800) 327-2012
Web site: www.levlad.com

Wide variety of natural health and beauty products, including skin lotions, liquid drink supplements, and shampoos and conditioners.

## NEEDS, Inc.

P.O. Box 580
East Syracuse, NY 13057
(800) 634-1380
Web site: www.needs.com
e-mail: needs@needs.com

Provides air and water filtration systems, domestics (linens, etc.), cleaners, sealers, vitamins and supplements, health and beauty aids, books, and fragrance-free products for people with allergies or chemical sensitivities.

## Nigra Enterprises

5699 Kanan Road SCP
Agoura, CA 91301
(818) 889-6877

Vendor for air and water treatment appliances, saunas, and respiratory appliances for environmentally sensitive people.

## FOOD STORAGE AND EQUIPMENT

### The Chef's Catalog Co.

P.O. Box 620048
Dallas, TX 75262
(800) 338-3232 (orders)
(800) 967-2433 (customer service)
Web site: www.chefscatalog.com

Stainless steel bakeware and cookware, cookie molds, coffee makers, waffle makers, carbonated water dispensers, and toasters. Call for a catalog.

### Janice Corp.

198 U.S. Highway 46
Budd Lake, NJ 07828
(800) JANICES (800-526-4237)
e-mail: jswack@worldnet.att.net

Cellophane bags, 100% cotton potholders, towels, rugs, and other untreated, all-cotton products.

### The Living Source

P.O. Box 20155
Waco, TX 76702
(254) 776-4878
Voice Ordering Line: (800) 662-8787
Web site: www.livingsource.com
e-mail: livingsource@earthlink.net

Offers a wide variety of products for people with allergies or who have compromised immune systems. Provider of safe and unscented soaps, and air and water filters.

### Williams-Sonoma, Inc.

(800) 541-2233
Website: www.williams-sonoma.com

Variety of specialty equipment, including mesh soda siphon (and extra cartridges), cotton hand towels, and more. Their store locator is on their Web site. Or contact them for a catalog or to locate a store near you.

## FOODS

### Allergy Resources

301 East 57th Avenue, Suite D
Denver, CO 80216
(800) 873-3529

40-page catalog. Hypoallergenic laundry and dishwashing products; carpet cleaner; natural foods; teff, amaranth, buckwheat, oat, sorghum syrup and flour, spelt, rice, millet, Kamut brand grain, gluten-free flours; baking ingredients such as xanthan gum, agar powder, and arrowroot; alternative sweeteners such as white stevia powder; hypoallergenic bedding and pillows; and air purifiers.

### American Spoon Foods, Inc.

P.O. Box 566
Petoskey, MI 49770
(800) 222-5886
Web site: www.spoon.com
e-mail: information@spoon.com

Hickory nuts, fruit preserves or "spoon fruit" (jam without sugar), dried morel mushrooms, dried tart red cherries, full line of grilling sauces, salsas, and salad dressings; additive- and preservative-free.

### Chuck's Seafoods

P.O. Box 5502
Charleston, OR 97420-0613
(541) 888-5525

Pacific albacore tuna, shrimp, crab, and salmon, packed in glass or can; no salt, oils, or other additives.

### Czimer's Game and Sea Foods, Inc.

13136 W. 159th Street
Lockport, IL 60441
(708) 301-0500

Game-farm raised animals, including buffalo.
Not necessarily organic. For a brochure send self-
addressed stamped, business-size envelope.

### Ener-G Foods, Inc.

P.O. Box 84487
Seattle, WA 98124-5787
(800) 331-5222
Web site: www.ener-g.com

Extensive product line, including wheat-free
and gluten-free mixes that use rice flour,
potato flour, sweet rice flour, bean flour, and
tapioca and potato starch; also egg and milk
substitutes, pure rice pastas, and a large variety
of wheat-free baked goods such as pretzels and
crackers. Also xanthan gum and many other
products.

### Food for Life Baking Co., Inc.

P.O. Box 1434
Corona CA 92878-1434
2991 E. Doherty St.
Corona, CA 92879-5811
(800) 797-5090
Web site: www.food-for-life.com

Specializes in breads, buns, rolls, English
muffins, bagels, energy bars, pita breads, bran
muffins, cakes, cereals, and pastas, among
others. Each line includes products specifically
developed to meet particular dietary require-
ments. Special categories include organic, flour-
less, sprouted grain, high fiber, wheat-free,
gluten-free, low sodium, unsweetened, fruit juice
sweetened, dairy-free, low fat, and yeast-free
baked goods.

### Gluten Solutions, Inc.

737 Manhattan Beach Boulevard, Suite B
Manhattan Beach, CA 90266
(888) 8-GLUTEN (888-845-8836)
Web site: www.glutensolutions.com

Gluten-free products. Call for free catalog.

### Great River Milling

P.O. Box 73
Winona, MN 55987
(507) 457-0334
e-mail: gromnrb@hbci.com

Specializes in grinding bread flour, specialty
flour, pancake mixes, and hot cereal.

### Habbersett Co.

701 Ashland Avenue
Folcroft, PA 19032
(610) 532-9973

Pure pork sausage (no MSG or other additives).

### Hills Foods Ltd.

3650 Bonneville Place, Suite 109
Burnaby, B.C. Canada V3N 4T7
(604) 421-3100
Web site: www.hillsfoods.com
e-mail: sales@hillsfoods.com

Contact Hills Foods to find names of organic
game suppliers in the United States. They
supply organic meats, game meats, and
specialty poultry (squab, pheasants, quail)
to Canadians.

### Jaffe Bros. Natural Foods

P.O. Box 636
Valley Center, CA 92082-0636
(760) 749-1133
Web site: www.organicfruitsandnuts.com
e-mail: jb54@worldnet.att.net

Organically grown dried fruits, nuts, seeds, grains, beans, nut butters, honey, unrefined salad oils, Safari snack bars, carob confections, and many other natural foods.

## Mountain Ark Trading Co.

799 Old Leicester Highway
Asheville, NC 28806
(800) 643-8909
Web site: www.mountainark.com

Importers and purveyors of traditional and organic Japanese foods plus domestic natural and organic foods, such as macrobiotic foods, many grains, beans, nuts, seeds, nonwheat pastas, and sea vegetables (such as kombu); also offers spelt and teff flours.

## Nu-World Amaranth, Inc.

P.O. Box 2202
Naperville, IL 60567
(630) 369-6819
Web site: www.nuworldamaranth.com

Certified organic amaranth and quinoa, including whole-seed amaranth, fine amaranth flour, puffed amaranth, amaranth bran flour, amaranth flake cereal, amaranth/buckwheat pizza crust, puffed quinoa, and quinoa flour. Also flat bread made with garbanzo flour. Amaranth seeds available for garden planting (harvest leaves like spinach; they grow right back).

## Ottomanelli Brothers

1549 York Avenue
New York, NY 10028
(888) NYC-OTTO (888-692-6886)
Web site: www.ottomanellis.com

Wild game (chill-packed immediately after cutting; insulated and shipped by air freight).

## Pacific Bakery: Yeast-Free

P.O. Box 950
Oceanside, CA 92049-0950
(760) 757-6020
Web site: www.pacificbakery.com

Yeast-free organic breads and bagels. Made with no yeast, sugar, honey, eggs, dairy, baking powder, or baking soda. Sold in natural food stores nationwide and direct, with minimum order.

## Shiloh Farms

P.O. Box 97
Sulphur Springs, AR 72768-0097
(800) 362-6832
Web site: www.users.nwark.com/~shilohf

Sprouted grain breads, single flour breads, hearth breads, granolas, mixes, nuts, flours, legumes, meat, cereals, carob.

## Special Foods

9207 Shotgun Court
Springfield, VA 22153-1444
(703) 644-0991
Web site: www.specialfoods.com

Flours, cereals, pastas, and baked products for individuals with extensive food and chemical sensitivities.

## Sunrich, Inc.

3824 S.W. 93rd Street
Hope, MN 56046
e-mail: info@sunrich.com
Web site: www.sunrich.com

Organic cornmeal and oat flours.

## Willow Hill Farm

313 Hardscrabble Road
Milton, VT 05468
(802) 893-2963
Web site: www.sheepcheese.com
e-mail: wsmart.together.net

Maker of award-winning farmhouse sheep's- and cow's-milk cheeses and pasture-raised organic lambs.

## NUTRITIONAL SUPPLEMENTS

### Abrams Royal Pharmacy

8220 Abrams Road
Dallas, TX 75231
(800) 458-0804

A compounding pharmacy specializing in made-to-order medicines without the additives or dyes that may cause allergies. Also specializing in providing nutritious homeopathic supplements.

### Allergy Research Group/Nutricology, Inc.

30806 Santana Street
Hayward, CA 94544
(800) 545-9960
Web site: www.nutricology.com

Nutritional supplement line with over 300 products especially designed for sensitive and highly allergic individuals.

### Bronson Laboratories, Inc.

600 E. Quality Drive
American Fork, UT 84003-3302
(800) 235-3200
Web site: www.bronsononline.com

Full line of supplements (including vitamin C crystals) many of which are free of sugar, starch, wheat, soy, yeast, corn and artificial colors, flavors, and preservatives; contact for specific ingredient information.

### Carlson Laboratories, Inc.

15 College Drive
Arlington Heights, IL 60004-1985
(888) 234-5656
Web site: www.carlsonlabs.com
e-mail: carlson@carlsonlabs.com

Supplements free of artificial colors and preservatives, vitamin C crystals, several forms of vitamin E (one soy-based), vitamin A (beta carotene) from algae, several special formulations.

### College Pharmacy

3505 Austin Bluff Parkway
Suite 101
Colorado Springs, CO 80918
(800) 888-9358

Compounding pharmacy specializing in making estrogen/progesterone hormones and allergen injections.

### Freeda Vitamins, Inc.

36 East 41st Street
New York, NY 10017
(800) 777-3737
e-mail: freedavits@aol.com

Quick-dissolving vitamin C crystals (Dull-C); starch-free and sugar-free line of vegetarian supplements; yeast-free selenium; lactose-free acidophilus (approved by the Feingold Association and the Hypoglycemia Association, certified kosher). Free brochure available.

### L & H Vitamins, Inc.

32-33 47th Avenue
Long Island City, NY 11101
(800) 221-1152
Web site: www.vitamins.com

A selection of more than 10,000 nationally advertised vitamins and health products at 20 to 40 percent off retail; maintains VITA-BANK, a computerized database of ingredients in all nationally distributed brands of supplements.

**Serammune Physicians Laboratory**

14 Pidgeon Hill Drive, Suite 300
Sterling, VA 20165
(800) 553-5472

Laboratory services include the advanced cell technique, ELISA/ACT used in determining which foods or chemicals are reactive in food allergies.

**The Vitamin Shoppe**

Customer Care Department
4700 Westside Avenue
North Bergen, NJ 07047
(800) 223-1216
Web site: www.vitaminshoppe.com

Supplements that are free of sugar, yeast, dairy, soy, starches, and other additives; digestive aids, all at a 20 to 40 percent discount.

**Wellness, Health & Pharmaceuticals**

2800 South 18th Street
Birmingham, AL 35209-2510
(800) 227-2627
Web site: www.wellnesshealth.com

Compounding pharmacy for custom medications free of all major allergens. Also nutritional supplements and products for the environmentally and chemically sensitive; free of yeast, starch, sugar, dyes, etc.; prices 20 to 40 percent below retail.

# Index to Recipes for a Rotary Diversified Diet

The following reference aid is a handy short-cut to finding recipes in this book that are suitable for a Rotary Diversified Diet as well as those involving only three or four food families. Here are some additional tips to help limit the number of food families you will be exposed to in a given meal:

* Omit optional ingredients.

* Match the nuts or seeds used in a recipe with the oil used (for example, use sunflower seeds with sunflower oil, walnuts with walnut oil, and almonds with almond oil). Both ingredients, being from the same family, count as one food exposure from that family.

* Use canola and olive oils when there are no nuts or seeds in a recipe or if you react to nuts and seeds. Avocado oil is another non-nut or seed oil option that agrees with many people.

* Familiarize yourself with some of the larger food families so that you can choose two or more members of the same family (see "Food Families" on page 41). Examples: celery, carrots, and parsley are often used together in soups, stews, and salads. Or make a fresh fruit salad using plums, peaches, apricots, nectarines, and cherries—all from the Plum family. (And add almonds, if you like.)

* Use vitamin C crystals in place of lemon juice or vinegar. Vitamin C crystals (citric acid), as well as baking soda and salt, are freebies when counting food families. They are basic compounds, unrelated to any food family.

* Use water instead of stock, white wine, or fruit juice when given a choice. A water-based dish may lack the depth of flavor that stock, wine, or juice would bring to it, but these ingredients, especially stock, involve many food families. Make this choice based on what's important to you.

# General Index

Underscored page references indicate boxed text.

## A

# B

# C

# D

# G

# I

Ice Cream
  Maple-Pecan Ice Cream, 267
  Peach-Almond Ice Cream, 338–39
  Strawberry Ice Cream, 268
Iron, sources of, 57–58
Italian-style dishes
  Chicken Cacciatore, 217
  Chilled Pasta Salad with Cucumber-Dill
      Sauce, 171
  Creamy Pasta with Vegetables, 170
  Fettuccini with Spinach Pesto,
      168–69
  Gemelli with Leek-Pepper Sauce, 168
  Italian Crumbs, 134
  Italian Seasoning, 210
  Italian Spaghetti Sauce, 200
  Kale-Sausage Risotto, 161
  Kamut Spaghetti with Sage Cream Sauce,
      167
  Marinated Sicilian Salad, 182
  Minestrone, 145
  Pasta Primavera Alfredo, 166
  Pesto Pasta, 165
  Spaghetti Squash Italian-Style, 162
  Wheat-Free Pizza with Goat's-Milk Cheese,
      265
  Zucchini Lasagna with Lamb, 164–65
  Zucchini Pasta, 163

# J

Jicama, 28–29
  Morning-Glory Chicken, 216
  Spicy Jicama Slaw, 188
  Stir-Fried Jicama Chicken Dinner, 215

# K

Kale, 28–29
  cooking times for, 177
  Kale-Lentil Soup, 143
  Kale-Sausage Risotto, 161
Kamut brand flour
  cooking and baking with, 11
  Kamut Drop Biscuits, 119
  Kamut-Grain Bread, 131
  Kamut-Maple Cake, 315
  Spelt-Kamut Pie Crust, 324–25
  Spelt-Kamut Streusel Crumbs, 328
Kidney beans
  Cowboy Beans, 230
  Four-Bean Salad, 184–85
  Kidney-Bean Salad, 184
  Kidney-Bean Vegetarian Stew, 152–53
  Mexican Supper with Quinoa, 251
  Pork and Pepper Stew with Beans,
      154
  Southwestern Rice and Meat Casserole,
      160–61
  Spelt-Cashew Casserole, 260
  Vegetarian Chili, 250–51
Kohlrabi, 28–29
  cooking times for, 177
Kombu (kelp), 32–33

# L

Lamb
  Cassoulet, 227
  Chunky Lamb Stew, 151
  Easy Curry, 228
  Lamb Stew, 148–49
  Moussaka-Style Casserole, 226

# M

vitamin D in, 53
Zucchini Milk, 302

Mint
Mint Sauce, 208

Miso, 33–34
Vegetable-Miso Soup, 138

Molasses
in baked goods, 19

Mold, household, 65, 70

Monosodium glutamate (MSG), 21

Muffins
Fresh Apple Muffins, 110
Grain-Free Banana-Nut Muffins, 111
Grain-Free Blueberry Muffins, 113
Oat Bran Muffins, 114
Pineapple-Cranberry Muffins with Quinoa, 112
Pumpkin Spice Muffins, 112–13
Rhubarb Oat-and-Rice Muffins, 115
as snacks and desserts, <u>116</u>

Mung beans
Mung-Bean Chowder, 373

Mushrooms, 30–31
Creamy Mushroom Soup, 140
Kamut Spaghetti with Sage Cream Sauce, 167
Marinated Sicilian Salad, 182
Mushroom Brown Sauce, 204
Mushroom-Rice Casserole, 160

Mustard
Creamy Mustard Sauce, 197
Tofu-Dijon Spread, 194

# N

Nut butters
Blond Fudge, 269
Carob–Nut Butter Fudge, 364

Carob-Nut Fudge Topping, 345
Hidden Treasures, 363
Kids' Delight Sandwich Spread, 279
Stuffed Dates, 298

Nutritional supplements, sources of, 385–87

Nutrition basics, 52–59

Nut(s). *See also specific nuts*
Carob–Nut Butter Fudge, 364
Fancy Berries and Nuts, 337
flours, cooking and baking with, 12–13
milks, 4
Mix-and-Match Breakfast Pudding, 105
Nut and Seed Crunch Crust, 327
Nutty Crème Topping, 345
Pineapple-Nut Shake, 303
protein in, 52
Sweet Nut Milk, 302

# O

Oat bran
Breakfast Oats Plus, 100
Oat Bran Muffins, 114
Oatmeal Patty Cakes, 97
Wheat-Free Oat-Bran Bread, 132

Oat flour, 13
Oat Crackers, 285
Rhubarb Oat-and-Rice Muffins, 115

Oats, rolled
Breakfast Oats Plus, 100
Carrot Survival Bars, 370
Easy Macaroons, 294
High-Fiber Cookies with Sesame Seeds, 294–95
High-Protein Granola, 102
No-Bake Granola, 368
Oat and Barley Scones, 117

# T

# V

# W

# Conversion Chart

These equivalents have been slightly rounded to make measuring easier.

## Volume Measurements

| U.S. | Imperial | Metric |
|------|----------|--------|
| ¼ tsp | – | 1 ml |
| ½ tsp | – | 2 ml |
| 1 tsp | – | 5 ml |
| 1 Tbsp | – | 15 ml |
| 2 Tbsp (1 oz) | 1 fl oz | 30 ml |
| ¼ cup (2 oz) | 2 fl oz | 60 ml |
| ⅓ cup (3 oz) | 3 fl oz | 80 ml |
| ½ cup (4 oz) | 4 fl oz | 120 ml |
| ⅔ cup (5 oz) | 5 fl oz | 160 ml |
| ¾ cup (6 oz) | 6 fl oz | 180 ml |
| 1 cup (8 oz) | 8 fl oz | 240 ml |

## Weight Measurements

| U.S. | Metric |
|------|--------|
| 1 oz | 30 g |
| 2 oz | 60 g |
| 4 oz (¼ lb) | 115 g |
| 5 oz (⅓ lb) | 145 g |
| 6 oz | 170 g |
| 7 oz | 200 g |
| 8 oz (½ lb) | 230 g |
| 10 oz | 285 g |
| 12 oz (¾ lb) | 340 g |
| 14 oz | 400 g |
| 16 oz (1 lb) | 455 g |
| 2.2 lb | 1 kg |

## Length Measurements

| U.S. | Metric |
|------|--------|
| ¼" | 0.6 cm |
| ½" | 1.25 cm |
| 1" | 2.5 cm |
| 2" | 5 cm |
| 4" | 11 cm |
| 6" | 15 cm |
| 8" | 20 cm |
| 10" | 25 cm |
| 12" (1') | 30 cm |

## Pan Sizes

| U.S. | Metric |
|------|--------|
| 8" cake pan | 20 × 4 cm sandwich or cake tin |
| 9" cake pan | 23 × 3.5 cm sandwich or cake tin |
| 11" × 7" baking pan | 28 × 18 cm baking tin |
| 13" × 9" baking pan | 32.5 × 23 cm baking tin |
| 15" × 10" baking pan | 38 × 25.5 cm baking tin (Swiss roll tin) |
| 1½ qt baking dish | 1.5 liter baking dish |
| 2 qt baking dish | 2 liter baking dish |
| 2 qt rectangular baking dish | 30 × 19 cm baking dish |
| 9" pie plate | 22 × 4 or 23 × 4 cm pie plate |
| 7" or 8" springform pan | 18 or 20 cm springform or loose-bottom cake tin |
| 9" × 5" loaf pan | 23 × 13 cm or 2 lb narrow loaf tin or pâté tin |

## Temperatures

| Fahrenheit | Centigrade | Gas |
|-----------|-----------|-----|
| 140° | 60° | – |
| 160° | 70° | – |
| 180° | 80° | – |
| 225° | 110° | – |
| 250° | 120° | ½ |
| 300° | 150° | 2 |
| 325° | 160° | 3 |
| 350° | 180° | 4 |
| 375° | 190° | 5 |
| 400° | 200° | 6 |
| 450° | 230° | 8 |
| 500° | 260° | – |